True Grit

**Center Point
Large Print**

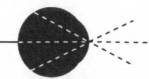

**This Large Print Book carries the
Seal of Approval of N.A.V.H.**

True Grit

WITHDRAWN

Charles Portis

CENTER POINT PUBLISHING
THORNDIKE, MAINE

This Center Point Large Print edition
is published in the year 2010 by arrangement with
Simon & Schuster, Inc.

True Grit appeared in a somewhat different version
in the *Saturday Evening Post*.

The text of this Large Print edition is unabridged.
In other aspects, this book may vary
from the original edition.
Printed in the United States of America
on permanent paper.
Set in 16-point Times New Roman type.

ISBN: 978-1-60285-937-1

Library of Congress Cataloging-in-Publication Data

Portis, Charles.
  True grit / Charles Portis.
    p. cm.
  ISBN 978-1-60285-937-1 (library binding : alk. paper)
  1. Teenage girls—Fiction. 2. Fathers—Death—Fiction.
  3. United States marshals—Fiction. 4. Outlaws—Fiction. 5. Revenge—Fiction.
  6. Large type books. I. Title.
  PS3566.O663T78 2010
  813'.54—dc22
                                                  2010028297

For my mother and father

PEOPLE DO not give it credence that a fourteen-year-old girl could leave home and go off in the wintertime to avenge her father's blood but it did not seem so strange then, although I will say it did not happen every day. I was just fourteen years of age when a coward going by the name of Tom Chaney shot my father down in Fort Smith, Arkansas, and robbed him of his life and his horse and one hundred and fifty dollars in cash money plus two California gold pieces that he carried in his trouser band.

Here is what happened. We had clear title to four hundred and eighty acres of good bottom land on the south bank of the Arkansas River not far from Dardanelle in Yell County, Arkansas. Tom Chaney was a tenant but working for hire and not on shares. He turned up one day hungry and riding a gray horse that had a filthy blanket on his back and a rope halter instead of a bridle. Papa took pity on the fellow and gave him a job and a place to live. It was a cotton house made over into a little cabin. It had a good roof.

Tom Chaney said he was from Louisiana. He was a short man with cruel features. I will tell more about his face later. He carried a Henry rifle. He was a bachelor about twenty-five years of age.

In November when the last of the cotton was

sold Papa took it in his head to go to Fort Smith and buy some ponies. He had heard that a stock trader there named Colonel Stonehill had bought a large parcel of cow ponies from Texas drovers on their way to Kansas and was now stuck with them. He was getting shed of them at bargain rates as he did not want to feed them over the winter. People in Arkansas did not think much of Texas mustang ponies. They were little and mean. They had never had anything but grass to eat and did not weigh over eight hundred pounds.

Papa had an idea they would make good deer-hunting ponies, being hardy and small and able to keep up with the dogs through the brush. He thought he would buy a small string of them and if things worked out he would breed and sell them for that purpose. His head was full of schemes. Anyway, it would be a cheap enough investment to start with, and we had a patch of winter oats and plenty of hay to see the ponies through till spring when they could graze in our big north pasture and feed on greener and juicier clover than they ever saw in the "Lone Star State." As I recollect, shelled corn was something under fifteen cents a bushel then.

Papa intended for Tom Chaney to stay and look after things on the place while he was gone. But Chaney set up a fuss to go and after a time he got the best of Papa's good nature. If Papa had a failing it was his kindly disposition. People would use him. I did not get my mean streak from him. Frank Ross was the gentlest, most honorable man who ever lived. He had a common-school education. He was a Cumberland Presbyterian and a Mason and he fought with determination at the battle of Elkhorn Tavern but was not wounded in that "scrap" as Lucille Biggers Langford states in her *Yell County Yesterdays*. I think I am in a position to know the facts. He was hurt in the terrible fight at Chickamauga up in the state of Tennessee and came near to dying on the way home from want of proper care.

Before Papa left for Fort Smith he arranged for a colored man named Yarnell Poindexter to feed the stock and look in on Mama and us every day. Yarnell and his family lived just below us on some land he rented from the bank. He was born of free parents in Illinois but a man named Bloodworth kidnapped him in Missouri and brought him down to Arkansas just before the war. Yarnell was a good man, thrifty and industrious, and he later became a prosperous house painter in Memphis, Tennessee. We exchanged letters every Christmas until he passed away in the flu epidemic of 1918. To this day I have never met anybody else named Yarnell, white or black. I attended the funeral and visited in Memphis with my brother, Little Frank, and his family.

Instead of going to Fort Smith by steamboat or train, Papa decided he would go on horseback and walk the ponies back all tied together. Not only would it be cheaper but it would be a pleasant outing for him and a good ride. Nobody loved to gad about on a prancing steed more than Papa. I have never been very fond of horses myself although I believe I was accounted a good enough rider in my youth. I never was afraid of animals. I remember once I rode a mean goat through a plum thicket on a dare.

From our place to Fort Smith was about seventy miles as a bird flies, taking you past beautiful Mount Nebo where we had a little summer house so Mama could get away from the mosquitoes, and also Mount Magazine, the highest point in Arkansas, but it might as well have been seven hundred miles for all I knew of Fort Smith. The boats went up there and some people sold their cotton up there but that was all I knew about it. We sold our cotton down in Little Rock. I had been there two or three times.

Papa left us on his saddle horse, a big chestnut mare with a blazed face called Judy. He took some food and a change of clothes rolled up in some blankets and covered with a slicker. This was tied behind his saddle. He wore his belt gun which was a big long dragoon pistol, the cap-and-ball kind that was old-fashioned even at that time. He had carried it in the war. He was a handsome sight and in my memory's eye I can still see him mounted up there on Judy in his brown woolen coat and black

Sunday hat and the both of them, man and beast, blowing little clouds of steam on that frosty morn. He might have been a gallant knight of old. Tom Chaney rode his gray horse that was better suited to pulling a middlebuster than carrying a rider. He had no hand gun but he carried his rifle slung across his back on a piece of cotton plow line. There is trash for you. He could have taken an old piece of harness and made a nice leather strap for it. That would have been too much trouble.

Papa had right around two hundred and fifty dollars in his purse as I had reason to know since I kept his books for him. Mama was never any good at sums and she could hardly spell cat. I do not boast of my own gifts in that direction. Figures and letters are not everything. Like Martha I have always been agitated and troubled by the cares of the day but my mother had a serene and loving heart. She was like Mary and had chosen "that good part." The two gold pieces that Papa carried concealed in his clothes were a marriage gift from my Grandfather Spurling in Monterey, California.

Little did Papa realize that morning that he was never to see us or hold us again, nor would he ever again harken to the meadowlarks of Yell County trilling a joyous anthem to spring.

The news came like a thunderclap. Here is what happened. Papa and Tom Chaney arrived in Fort Smith and took a room at the Monarch boardinghouse. They called on Stonehill at his stock barn and looked over the ponies. It fell out that there was not a mare in the lot, or a stallion for that matter. The Texas cow-boys rode nothing but geldings for some cow-boy reason of their own and you can imagine they are no good for breeding purposes. But Papa was not to be turned back. He was determined to own some of those little brutes and on the second day he bought four of them for one hundred dollars even, bringing Stonehill down from his asking price of one hundred and forty dollars. It was a good enough buy.

They made plans to leave the next morning. That night Tom Chaney went to a barroom and got into a game of cards with some "riffraff" like himself and lost his wages. He did not take the loss like a man but went back to the room at the boardinghouse and sulled up like a possum. He had a bottle of whiskey and he drank that. Papa was sitting in the parlor talking to some drummers. By and by Chaney came out of the bedroom with his rifle. He said he had been cheated and was going back to the barroom and get his money. Papa said if he had been cheated then they had best go talk to the law about it. Chaney would not listen. Papa followed him outside and told him to surrender the rifle as he was in no fit state to start a quarrel with a gun in his hand. My father was not armed at that time.

Tom Chaney raised his rifle and shot him in the forehead, killing him instantly. There was no more provocation than that and I tell it as it was told to me by the high sheriff of Sebastian County. Some people might say, well, what business was it of Frank Ross to meddle? My answer is this: he was trying to do that short devil a good turn. Chaney was a tenant and Papa felt responsibility. He was his brother's keeper. Does that answer your question?

Now the drummers did not rush out to grab Chaney or shoot him but instead scattered like poultry while Chaney took my father's purse from his warm body and ripped open the trouser band and took the gold pieces too. I cannot say how he knew about them. When he finished his thieving he raced to the end of the street and struck the night watchman at the stock barn a fierce blow to the mouth with his rifle stock, knocking him silly. He put a bridle on Papa's horse Judy and rode out bareback. Darkness swallowed him up. He might have taken the time to saddle the horse or hitched up three spans of mules to a Concord stagecoach and smoked a pipe as it seems no one in that city was after him. He had mistaken the drummers for men. "The wicked flee when none pursueth."

LAWYER DAGGETT had gone to Helena to try one of his steamboat suits and so Yarnell and I rode the train to Fort Smith to see about Papa's body. I took around one hundred dollars expense money and wrote myself out a letter of identification and signed Lawyer Daggett's name to it and had Mama sign it as well. She was in bed.

There were no seats to be had on the coaches. The reason for this was that there was to be a triple hanging at the Federal Courthouse in Fort Smith and people from as far away as east Texas and north Louisiana were going up to see it. It was like an excursion trip. We rode in a colored coach and Yarnell got us a trunk to sit on.

When the conductor came through he said, "Get that trunk out of the aisle, nigger!"

I replied to him in this way: "We will move the trunk but there is no reason for you to be so hateful about it."

He did not say anything to that but went on taking tickets. He saw that I had brought to all the darkies' attention how little he was. We stood up all the way but I was young and did not mind. On the way we had a good lunch of spare ribs that Yarnell had brought along in a sack.

I noticed that the houses in Fort Smith were numbered but it was no city at all compared to

Little Rock. I thought then and still think that Fort Smith ought to be in Oklahoma instead of Arkansas, though of course it was not Oklahoma across the river then but the Indian Territory. They have that big wide street there called Garrison Avenue like places out in the west. The buildings are made of fieldstone and all the windows need washing. I know many fine people live in Fort Smith and they have one of the nation's most modern waterworks but it does not look like it belongs in Arkansas to me.

There was a jailer at the sheriff's office and he said we would have to talk to the city police or the high sheriff about the particulars of Papa's death. The sheriff had gone to the hanging. The undertaker was not open. He had left a notice on his door saying he would be back after the hanging. We went to the Monarch boardinghouse but there was no one there except a poor old woman with cataracts on her eyes. She said everybody had gone to the hanging but her. She would not let us in to see about Papa's traps. At the city police station we found two officers but they were having a fist fight and were not available for inquiries.

Yarnell wanted to see the hanging but he did not want me to go so he said we should go back to the sheriff's office and wait there until everybody got back. I did not much care to see it but I saw he wanted to so I said no, we would go to the hanging but I would not tell Mama about it. That was what he was worried about.

The Federal Courthouse was up by the river on a little rise and the big gallows was hard beside it. About a thousand or more people and fifty or sixty dogs had gathered there to see the show. I believe a year or two later they put up a wall around the place and you had to have a pass from the marshal's office to get in but at this time it was open to the public. A noisy boy was going through the crowd selling parched peanuts and fudge. Another one was selling "hot tamales" out of a bucket. This is a cornmeal tube filled with spicy meat that they eat in Old Mexico. They are not bad. I had never seen one before.

When we got there the preliminaries were just about over. Two white men and an Indian were standing up there on the platform with their hands tied behind them and the three nooses hanging loose beside their heads. They were all wearing new jeans and flannel shirts buttoned at the neck. The hangman was a thin bearded man named George Maledon. He was wearing two long pistols. He was a Yankee and they say he would not hang a man who had been in the G.A.R. A marshal read the sentences but his voice was low and we could not make out what he was saying. We pushed up closer.

A man with a Bible talked to each of the men for a minute. I took him for a preacher. He led them in

16

singing "Amazing Grace, How Sweet the Sound" and some people in the crowd joined in. Then Maledon put the nooses on their necks and tightened up the knots just the way he wanted them. He went to each man with a black hood and asked him if he had any last words before he put it on him.

The first one was a white man and he looked put out by it all but not upset as you might expect from a man in his desperate situation. He said, "Well, I killed the wrong man and that is why I am here. If I had killed the man I meant to I don't believe I would have been convicted. I see men out there in that crowd that is worse than me."

The Indian was next and he said, "I am ready. I have repented my sins and soon I will be in heaven with Christ my savior. Now I must die like a man." If you are like me you probably think of Indians as heathens. But I will ask you to recall the thief on the cross. He was never baptized and never even heard of a catechism and yet Christ himself promised him a place in heaven.

The last one had a little speech ready. You could tell he had learned it by heart. He had long yellow hair. He was older than the other two, being around thirty years of age. He said, "Ladies and gentlemen, my last thoughts are of my wife and my two dear little boys who are far away out on the Cimarron River. I don't know what is to become of them. I hope and pray that people will not slight

17

them and compel them to go into low company on account of the disgrace I have brought them. You see what I have come to because of drink. I killed my best friend in a trifling quarrel over a pocketknife. I was drunk and it could just as easily have been my brother. If I had received good instruction as a child I would be with my family today and at peace with my neighbors. I hope and pray that all you parents in the sound of my voice will train up your children in the way they should go. Thank you. Goodbye everyone."

He was in tears and I am not ashamed to own that I was too. The man Maledon covered his head with the hood and went to his lever. Yarnell put a hand over my face but I pushed it aside. I would see it all. With no more ado Maledon sprung the trap and the hinged doors fell open in the middle and the three killers dropped to judgment with a bang. A noise went up from the crowd as though they had been struck a blow. The two white men gave no more signs of life. They spun slowly around on the tight creaking ropes. The Indian jerked his legs and arms up and down in spasms. That was the bad part and many in the crowd turned in revulsion and left in some haste, and we were among them.

We were told that the Indian's neck had not been broken, as was the case with the other two, and that he swung there and strangled for more than a half hour before a doctor pronounced him dead and had him lowered. They say the Indian had lost weight in jail and was too light for a proper job. I have since learned that Judge Isaac Parker watched all his hangings from an upper window in the Courthouse. I suppose he did this from a sense of duty. There is no knowing what is in a man's heart.

Perhaps you can imagine how painful it was for us to go directly from that appalling scene to the undertaker's where my father lay dead. Nevertheless it had to be done. I have never been one to flinch or crawfish when faced with an unpleasant task. The undertaker was an Irishman. He took Yarnell and me to a room at the back that was very dark owing to the windows being painted green. The Irishman was courteous and sympathetic but I did not much like the coffin he had placed Papa in. It was resting on three low stools and was made of pine planks that had not been cleanly dressed. Yarnell took off his hat.

The Irishman said, "And is that the man?" He held a candle in his face. The body was wrapped in a white shroud.

I said, "That is my father." I stood there looking at him. What a waste! Tom Chaney would pay for this! I would not rest easy until that Louisiana cur was roasting and screaming in hell!

The Irishman said, "If ye would loike to kiss him it will be all roight."

I said, "No, put the lid on it."

We went to the man's office and I signed some

coroner's papers. The charge for the coffin and the embalming was something over sixty dollars. The shipping charge to Dardanelle was nine dollars and fifty cents.

Yarnell took me outside the office. He said, "Miss Mattie, that man trying to stick you."

I said, "Well, we will not haggle with him."

He said, "That is what he counting on."

I said, "We will let it go."

I paid the Irishman his money and got a receipt. I told Yarnell to stay with the coffin and see that it was loaded on the train with care and not handled roughly by some thoughtless railroad hand.

I went to the sheriff's office. The high sheriff was friendly and he gave me the full particulars on the shooting, but I was disappointed to learn how little had been done toward the apprehension of Tom Chaney. They had not even got his name right.

The sheriff said, "We do know this much. He was a short man but well set up. He had a black mark on his cheek. His name is Chambers. He is now over in the Territory and we think he was in the party with Lucky Ned Pepper that robbed a mail hack Tuesday down on the Poteau River."

I said, "That is the description of Tom Chaney. There is no Chambers to it. He got that black mark in Louisiana when a man shot a pistol in his face and the powder got under the skin. Anyhow, that is his story. I know him and can identify him. Why are you not out looking for him?"

The sheriff said, "I have no authority in the Indian Nation. He is now the business of the U.S. marshals."

I said, "When will they arrest him?"

He said, "It is hard to say. They will have to catch him first."

I said, "Do you know if they are even after him?"

He said, "Yes, I have asked for a fugitive warrant and I expect there is a Federal John Doe warrant on him now for the mail robbery. I will inform the marshals as to the correct name."

"I will inform them myself," said I. "Who is the best marshal they have?"

The sheriff thought on it for a minute. He said, "I would have to weigh that proposition. There is near about two hundred of them. I reckon William Waters is the best tracker. He is a half-breed Comanche and it is something to see, watching him cut for sign. The meanest one is Rooster Cogburn. He is a pitiless man, double-tough, and fear don't enter into his thinking. He loves to pull a cork. Now L. T. Quinn, he brings his prisoners in alive. He may let one get by now and then but he believes even the worst of men is entitled to a fair shake. Also the court does not pay any fees for dead men. Quinn is a good peace officer and a lay preacher to boot. He will not plant evidence or abuse a prisoner. He is straight as a string. Yes, I will say Quinn is about the best they have."

I said, "Where can I find this Rooster?"

He said, "You will probably find him in Federal Court tomorrow. They will be trying that Wharton boy."

The sheriff had Papa's gun belt there in a drawer and he gave it to me in a sugar sack to carry. The clothes and blankets were at the boardinghouse. The man Stonehill had the ponies and Papa's saddle at his stock barn. The sheriff wrote me out a note for the man Stonehill and the landlady at the boardinghouse, who was a Mrs. Floyd. I thanked him for his help. He said he wished he could do more.

It was around five-thirty P.M. when I got to the depot. The days were growing short and it was already dark. The southbound train was to leave some few minutes after six o'clock. I found Yarnell waiting outside the freight car where he had loaded the coffin. He said the express agent had consented to let him ride in the car with the coffin.

He said he would go help me find a seat in a coach but I said, "No, I will stay over a day or two. I must see about those ponies and I want to make sure the law is on the job. Chaney has got clean away and they are not doing much about it."

Yarnell said, "You can't stay in this city by yourself."

I said, "It will be all right. Mama knows I can take care of myself. Tell her I will be stopping at the Monarch boardinghouse. If there is no room there I will leave word with the sheriff where I am."

He said, "I reckon I will stay too."

I said, "No, I want you to go with Papa. When you get home tell Mr. Myers I said to put him in a better coffin."

"Your mama will not like this," said he.

"I will be back in a day or two. Tell her I said not to sign anything until I get home. Have you had anything to eat?"

"I had me a cup of hot coffee. I ain't hongry."

"Do they have a stove in that car?"

"I will be all right wrapped in my coat."

"I sure do appreciate this, Yarnell."

"Mr. Frank was always mighty good to me."

Some people will take it wrong and criticize me for not going to my father's funeral. My answer is this: I had my father's business to attend to. He was buried in his Mason's apron by the Danville lodge.

I got to the Monarch in time to eat. Mrs. Floyd said she had no vacant room because of the big crowd in town but that she would put me up somehow. The daily rate was seventy-five cents a night with two meals and a dollar with three meals. She did not have a rate for one meal so I was obliged to give her seventy-five cents even though I had planned to buy some cheese and crackers the next morning for my daytime eats. I don't know what her weekly rate was.

There were ten or twelve people at the supper table and all men except for me and Mrs. Floyd and the poor old blind woman who was called "Grandma Turner." Mrs. Floyd was a right big talker. She explained to everybody that I was the daughter of the man who had been shot in front of her house. I did not appreciate it. She told about the event in detail and asked me impertinent questions about my family. It was all I could do to reply politely. I did not wish to discuss the thing with idly curious strangers, no matter how well intentioned they might be.

I sat at one corner of the table between her and a tall, long-backed man with a doorknob head and a mouthful of prominent teeth. He and Mrs. Floyd did most of the talking. He traveled about selling pocket calculators. He was the only man there wearing a suit of clothes and a necktie. He told some interesting stories about his experiences but the others paid little attention to him, being occupied with their food like hogs rooting in a bucket.

"Watch out for those chicken and dumplings," he told me.

Some of the men stopped eating.

"They will hurt your eyes," he said.

A dirty man across the table in a smelly deerskin coat said, "How is that?"

With a mischievous twinkle the drummer replied, "They will hurt your eyes looking for the chicken." I thought it a clever joke but the dirty man said angrily, "You squirrelheaded son of a bitch," and went back to eating. The drummer kept quiet after that. The dumplings were all right but I could not see twenty-five cents in a little flour and grease.

After supper some of the men left to go to town, probably to drink whiskey in the barrooms and listen to the hurdy-gurdy. The rest of us went to the parlor. The boarders dozed and read newspapers and talked about the hanging and the drummer told yellow fever jokes. Mrs. Floyd brought out Papa's things that were bundled in the slicker and I went through them and made an inventory.

Everything seemed to be there, even his knife and watch. The watch was of brass and not very expensive but I was surprised to find it because people who will not steal big things will often steal little things like that. I stayed in the parlor and listened to the talk for a while and then asked Mrs. Floyd if she would show me to my bed.

She said, "Go straight down that hall to the last bedroom on the left. There is a bucket of water and a washpan on the back porch. The toilet is out back directly behind the chinaberry tree. You will be sleeping with Grandma Turner."

She must have seen the dismay on my face for she added, "It will be all right. Grandma Turner will not mind. She is used to doubling up. She will not even know you are there, sweet."

Since I was the paying customer I believed my wishes should have been considered before

Grandma Turner's, though it seemed neither of us was to have any say.

Mrs. Floyd went on, saying, "Grandma Turner is a sound sleeper. It is certainly a blessing at her age. Do not worry about waking Grandma Turner, a little mite like you."

I did not mind sleeping with Grandma Turner but I thought Mrs. Floyd had taken advantage of me. Still, I saw nothing to be gained from making a fuss at that hour. She already had my money and I was tired and it was too late to look for lodging elsewhere.

The bedroom was cold and dark and smelled like medicine. A wintry blast came up through the cracks in the floor. Grandma Turner turned out to be more active in her slumber than I had been led to expect. When I got into bed I found she had all the quilts on her side. I pulled them over. I said my prayers and was soon asleep. I awoke to find that Grandma Turner had done the trick again. I was bunched up in a knot and trembling with cold from the exposure. I pulled the covers over again. This happened once more later in the night and I got up, my feet freezing, and arranged Papa's blankets and slicker over me as makeshift covers. Then I slept all right.

MRS. FLOYD served me no meat for breakfast, only grits and a fried egg. After eating I put the watch and knife in my pocket and took the gun along in the sugar sack.

At the Federal Courthouse I learned that the head marshal had gone to Detroit, Michigan, to deliver prisoners to the "house of correction," as they called it. A deputy who worked in the office said they would get around to Tom Chaney in good time, but that he would have to wait his turn. He showed me a list of indicted outlaws that were then on the loose in the Indian Territory and it looked like the delinquent tax list that they run in the *Arkansas Gazette* every year in little type. I did not like the looks of that, nor did I care much for the "smarty" manner of the deputy. He was puffed up by his office. You can expect that out of Federal people and to make it worse this was a Republican gang that cared nothing for the opinion of the good people of Arkansas who are Democrats.

In the courtroom itself they were empaneling a jury. The bailiff at the door told me that the man Rooster Cogburn would be around later in the day when the trial began as he was the main witness for the prosecution.

I went to Stonehill's stock barn. He had a nice

barn and behind it a big corral and a good many small feeder pens. The bargain cow ponies, around thirty head, all colors, were in the corral. I thought they would be broken-down scrubs but they were frisky things with clear eyes and their coats looked healthy enough, though dusty and matted. They had probably never known a brush. They had burrs in their tails.

I had hated these ponies for the part they played in my father's death but now I realized the notion was fanciful, that it was wrong to charge blame to these pretty beasts who knew neither good nor evil but only innocence. I say that of these ponies. I have known some horses and a good many more pigs who I believe harbored evil intent in their hearts. I will go further and say all cats are wicked, though often useful. Who has not seen Satan in their sly faces? Some preachers will say, well, that is superstitious "claptrap." My answer is this: Preacher, go to your Bible and read Luke 8:26–33.

Stonehill had an office in one corner of the barn. On the door glass it said, "Col. G. Stonehill. Licensed Auctioneer. Cotton Factor." He was in there behind his desk and he had a red-hot stove going. He was a prissy baldheaded man with eyeglasses.

I said, "How much are you paying for cotton?"

He looked up at me and said, "Nine and a half for low middling and ten for ordinary."

I said, "We got most of ours out early and sold it

28

to Woodson Brothers in Little Rock for eleven cents."

He said, "Then I suggest you take the balance of it to the Woodson Brothers."

"We have sold it all," said I. "We only got ten and a half on the last sale."

"Why did you come here to tell me this?"

"I thought we might shop around up here next year, but I guess we are doing all right in Little Rock." I showed him the note from the sheriff. After he had read it he was not disposed to be so short with me.

He took off his eyeglasses and said, "It was a tragic thing. May I say your father impressed me with his manly qualities. He was a close trader but he acted the gentleman. My watchman had his teeth knocked out and can take only soup."

I said, "I am sorry to hear it."

He said, "The killer has flown to the Territory and is now on the scout there."

"This is what I heard."

"He will find plenty of his own stamp there," said he. "Birds of a feather. It is a sink of crime. Not a day goes by but there comes some new report of a farmer bludgeoned, a wife outraged, or a blameless traveler set upon and cut down in a sanguinary ambuscade. The civilizing arts of commerce do not flourish there."

I said, "I have hopes that the marshals will get him soon. His name is Tom Chaney. He worked for us. I am trying to get action. I aim to see him shot or hanged."

"Yes, yes, well might you labor to that end," said Stonehill. "At the same time I will counsel patience. The brave marshals do their best but they are few in number. The lawbreakers are legion and they range over a vast country that offers many natural hiding places. The marshal travels about friendless and alone in that criminal nation. Every man's hand is against him there save in large part for that of the Indian who has been cruelly imposed upon by felonious intruders from the States."

I said, "I would like to sell those ponies back to you that my father bought."

He said, "I fear that is out of the question. I will see that they are shipped to you at my earliest convenience."

I said, "We don't want the ponies now. We don't need them."

"That hardly concerns me," said he. "Your father bought these ponies and paid for them and there is an end of it. I have the bill of sale. If I had any earthly use for them I might consider an offer but I have already lost money on them and, be assured, I do not intend to lose more. I will be happy to accommodate you in shipping them. The popular steamer *Alice Waddell* leaves tomorrow for Little Rock. I will do what I can to find space on it for you and the stock."

I said, "I want three hundred dollars for Papa's saddle horse that was stolen."

He said, "You will have to take that up with the man who has the horse."

"Tom Chaney stole it while it was in your care," said I. "You are responsible."

Stonehill laughed at that. He said, "I admire your sand but I believe you will find I am not liable for such claims. Let me say too that your valuation of the horse is high by about two hundred dollars."

I said, "If anything, my price is low. Judy is a fine racing mare. She has won purses of twenty-five dollars at the fair. I have seen her jump an eight-rail fence with a heavy rider."

"All very interesting, I'm sure," said he.

"Then you will offer nothing?"

"Nothing except what is yours. The ponies are yours, take them. Your father's horse was stolen by a murderous criminal. This is regrettable but I had provided reasonable protection for the animal as per the implicit agreement with the client. We must each of us bear our own misfortunes. Mine is that I have temporarily lost the services of my watchman."

"I will take it to law," said I.

"You must do as you think best," said he.

"We will see if a widow and her three small children can get fair treatment in the courts of this city."

"You have no case."

"Lawyer J. Noble Daggett of Dardanelle, Arkansas, may think otherwise. Also a jury."

"Where is your mother?"

"She is at home in Yell County looking after my sister Victoria and my brother Little Frank."

"You must fetch her then. I do not like to deal with children."

"You will not like it any better when Lawyer Daggett gets hold of you. He is a grown man."

"You are impudent."

"I do not wish to be, sir, but I will not be pushed about when I am in the right."

"I will take it up with my attorney."

"And I will take it up with mine. I will send him a message by telegraph and he will be here on the evening train. He will make money and I will make money and your lawyer will make money and you, Mr. Licensed Auctioneer, will foot the bill."

"I cannot make an agreement with a child. You are not accountable. You cannot be bound to a contract."

"Lawyer Daggett will back up any decision I make. You may rest easy on that score. You can confirm any agreement by telegraph."

"This is a damned nuisance!" he exclaimed. "How am I to get my work done? I have a sale tomorrow."

"There can be no settlement after I leave this office," said I. "It will go to law."

He worried with his eyeglasses for a minute and then said, "I will pay two hundred dollars to your father's estate when I have in my hand a letter from your lawyer absolving me of all liability from the beginning of the world to date. It must be signed by your lawyer and your mother and it must be notarized. The offer is more than liberal and I only make it to avoid the possibility of troublesome litigation. I should never have come here. They told me this town was to be the Pittsburgh of the Southwest."

I said, "I will take two hundred dollars for Judy, plus one hundred dollars for the ponies and twenty-five dollars for the gray horse that Tom Chaney left. He is easily worth forty dollars. That is three hundred and twenty-five dollars total."

"The ponies have no part in this," said he. "I will not buy them."

"Then I will keep the ponies and the price for Judy will be three hundred and twenty-five dollars."

Stonehill snorted. "I would not pay three hundred and twenty-five dollars for winged Pegasus, and that splayfooted gray does not even belong to you."

I said, "Yes, he does. Papa only let Tom Chaney have the use of him."

"My patience is wearing thin. You are an unnatural child. I will pay two hundred and twenty-five dollars and keep the gray horse. I don't want the ponies."

"I cannot settle for that."

"This is my last offer. Two hundred and fifty dollars. For that I get a release and I keep your father's saddle. I am also writing off a feed and stabling charge. The gray horse is not yours to sell."

"The saddle is not for sale. I will keep it. Lawyer Daggett can prove the ownership of the gray horse. He will come after you with a writ of replevin."

"All right, now listen very carefully as I will not bargain further. I will take the ponies back and keep the gray horse and settle for three hundred dollars. Now you must take that or leave it and I do not much care which it is."

I said, "I am sure Lawyer Daggett would not wish me to consider anything under three hundred and twenty-five dollars. What you get for that is everything except the saddle and you get out of a costly lawsuit as well. It will go harder if Lawyer Daggett makes the terms as he will include a generous fee for himself."

"Lawyer Daggett! Lawyer Daggett! Who is this famous pleader of whose name I was happily ignorant ten minutes ago?"

I said, "Have you ever heard of the Great Arkansas River, Vicksburg & Gulf Steamship Company?"

"I have done business with the G.A.V.&G.," said he.

"Lawyer Daggett is the man who forced them

into receivership," said I. "They tried to 'mess' with him. It was a feather in his cap. He is on familiar terms with important men in Little Rock. The talk is he will be governor one day."

"Then he is a man of little ambition," said Stonehill, "incommensurate with his capacity for making mischief. I would rather be a country road overseer in Tennessee than governor of this benighted state. There is more honor in it."

"If you don't like it here you should pack your traps and go back where you came from."

"Would that I could get out from under!" said he. "I would be aboard the Friday morning packet with a song of thanksgiving on my lips."

"People who don't like Arkansas can go to the devil!" said I. "What did you come here for?"

"I was sold a bill of goods."

"Three hundred and twenty-five dollars is my figure."

"I would like to have that in writing for what it is worth." He wrote out a short agreement. I read it over and made a change or two and he initialed the changes. He said, "Tell your lawyer to send the letter to me here at Stonehill's Livery Stable. When I have it in my hand I will remit the extortion money. Sign this."

I said, "I will have him send the letter to me at the Monarch boardinghouse. When you give me the money I will give you the letter. I will sign this instrument when you have given me twenty-five dollars as a token of your good faith." Stonehill gave me ten dollars and I signed the paper.

I went to the telegraph office. I tried to keep the message down but it took up almost a full blank setting forth the situation and what was needed. I told Lawyer Daggett to let Mama know I was well and would be home soon. I forget what it cost.

I bought some crackers and a piece of hoop cheese and an apple at a grocery store and sat on a nail keg by the stove and had a cheap yet nourishing lunch. You know what they say, "Enough is as good as a feast." When I had finished eating I returned to Stonehill's place and tried to give the apple core to one of the ponies. They all shied away and would have nothing to do with me or my gift. The poor things had probably never tasted an apple. I went inside the stock barn out of the wind and lay down on some oat sacks. Nature tells us to rest after meals and people who are too busy to heed that inner voice are often dead at the age of fifty years.

Stonehill came by on his way out wearing a little foolish Tennessee hat. He stopped and looked at me.

I said, "I am taking a short nap."

He said, "Are you quite comfortable?"

I said, "I wanted to get out of the wind. I figured you would not mind."

"I don't want you smoking cigarettes in here."

36

"I don't use tobacco."

"I don't want you punching holes in those sacks with your boots."

"I will be careful. Shut that door good when you go out."

I had not realized how tired I was. It was well up in the afternoon when I awoke. I was stiff and my nose had begun to drip, sure sign of a cold coming on. You should always be covered while sleeping. I dusted myself off and washed my face under a pump and picked up my gun sack and made haste to the Federal Courthouse.

When I got there I saw that another crowd had gathered, although not as big as the one the day before. My thought was: *What? Surely they are not having another hanging!* They were not. What had attracted the people this time was the arrival of two prisoner wagons from the Territory.

The marshals were unloading the prisoners and poking them sharply along with their Winchester repeating rifles. The men were all chained together like fish on a string. They were mostly white men but there were also some Indians and half-breeds and Negroes. It was awful to see but you must remember that these chained beasts were murderers and robbers and train wreckers and bigamists and counterfeiters, some of the most wicked men in the world. They had ridden the "hoot-owl trail" and tasted the fruits of evil and now justice had caught up with them to demand payment. You must pay for everything in this world one way and another. There is nothing free except the Grace of God. You cannot earn that or deserve it.

The prisoners who were already in the jail, which was in the basement of the Courthouse, commenced to shout and catcall through little barred windows at the new prisoners, saying, "Fresh fish!" and such like. Some of them used ugly expressions so that the women in the crowd turned their heads. I put my fingers in my ears and walked through the people up to the steps of the Courthouse and inside.

The bailiff at the door did not want to let me in the courtroom as I was a child but I told him I had business with Marshal Cogburn and held my ground. He saw I had spunk and he folded right up, not wanting me to cause a stir. He made me stand beside him just inside the door but that was all right because there were no empty seats anyway. People were even sitting on windowsills.

You will think it strange but I had scarcely heard of Judge Isaac Parker at that time, famous man that he was. I knew pretty well what was going on in my part of the world and I must have heard mention of him and his court but it made little impression on me. Of course we lived in his district but we had our own circuit courts to deal with killers and thieves. About the only outlaws in our country who ever went to Federal Court were "moonshiners" like old man Jerry Vick and his boys. Most of Judge Parker's customers came from the Indian Territory which was a refuge for desperadoes from all over the map.

Now I will tell you an interesting thing. For a long time there was no appeal from his court except to the President of the United States. They later changed that and when the Supreme Court started reversing him, Judge Parker was annoyed. He said those people up in Washington city did not understand the bloody conditions in the Territory. He called Solicitor-General Whitney, who was supposed to be on the judge's side, a "pardon broker" and said he knew no more of criminal law than he did of the hieroglyphics of the Great Pyramid. Well, for their part, those people up there said the judge was too hard and highhanded and too longwinded in his jury charges and they called his court "the Parker slaughterhouse." I don't know who was right. I know sixty-five of his marshals got killed. They had some mighty tough folks to deal with.

The judge was a tall big man with blue eyes and a brown billy-goat beard and he seemed to me to be old, though he was only around forty years of age at that time. His manner was grave. On his deathbed he asked for a priest and became a Catholic. That was his wife's religion. It was his own business and none of mine. If you had sentenced one hundred and sixty men to death and seen around eighty of them swing, then maybe at the last minute you would feel the need of some stronger medicine than the Methodists could make. It is something to think about. Toward the last, he said he didn't hang all those men, that the law had done it. When he died of dropsy in 1896 all the prisoners down there in that dark jail had a "jubilee" and the jailers had to put it down.

I have a newspaper record of a part of that Wharton trial and it is not an official transcript but it is faithful enough. I have used it and my memories to write a good historical article that I titled, *You will now listen to the sentence of the law, Odus Wharton, which is that you be hanged by the neck until you are dead, dead, dead! May God, whose laws you have broken and before whose dread tribunal you must appear, have mercy on your soul. Being a personal recollection of Isaac C. Parker, the famous Border Judge.*

But the magazines of today do not know a good story when they see one. They would rather print trash. They say my article is too long and "discursive." Nothing is too long or too short either if you have a true and interesting tale and what I call a "graphic" writing style combined with educational aims. I do not fool around with newspapers. They are always after me for historical write-ups but when the talk gets around to money the paper editors are most of them "cheap skates." They think because I have a little money I will be happy to fill up their Sunday columns just to see my name in print like Lucille Biggers Langford and Florence Mabry Whiteside. As the little colored boy says, *"Not none of me!"* Lucille and Florence can do as they please. The paper editors are great ones for reaping where they have not sown. Another game they have is to send reporters out to talk to you and get your stories free. I know the young reporters are not paid well and I would not mind helping those boys out with their "scoops" if they could ever get anything straight.

When I got in the courtroom there was a Creek Indian boy on the witness stand and he was speaking in his own tongue and another Indian was interpreting for him. It was slow going. I stood there through almost an hour of it before they called Rooster Cogburn to the stand.

I had guessed wrong as to which one he was, picking out a younger and slighter man with a badge on his shirt, and I was surprised when an old one-eyed jasper that was built along the lines of Grover Cleveland went up and was sworn. I say "old." He was about forty years of age. The floor boards squeaked under his weight. He was wearing a dusty black suit of clothes and when he sat down I saw that his badge was on his vest. It was a little silver circle with a star in it. He had a mustache like Cleveland too.

Some people will say, well there were more men in the country at that time who looked like

Cleveland than did not. Still, that is how he looked. Cleveland was once a sheriff himself. He brought a good deal of misery to the land in the Panic of '93 but I am not ashamed to own that my family supported him and has stayed with the Democrats right on through, up to and including Governor Alfred Smith, and not only because of Joe Robinson. Papa used to say that the only friends we had down here right after the war were the Irish Democrats in New York. Thad Stevens and the Republican gang would have starved us all out if they could. It is all in the history books. Now I will introduce Rooster by way of the transcript and get my story "back on the rails."

MR. BARLOW: State your name and occupation please.

MR. COGBURN: Reuben J. Cogburn. I am a deputy marshal for the U.S. District Court for the Western District of Arkansas having criminal jurisdiction over the Indian Territory.

MR. BARLOW: How long have you occupied such office?

MR. COGBURN: Be four years in March.

MR. BARLOW: On November second were you carrying out your official duties?

MR. COGBURN: I was, yes sir.

MR. BARLOW: Did something occur on that day out of the ordinary?

MR. COGBURN: Yes sir.

MR. BARLOW: Please describe in your own words what that occurrence was.

MR. COGBURN: Yes sir. Well, not long after dinner on that day we was headed back for Fort Smith from the Creek Nation and was about four miles west of Webbers Falls.

MR. BARLOW: One moment. Who was with you?

MR. COGBURN: There was four other deputy marshals and me. We had a wagonload of prisoners and was headed back for Fort Smith. Seven prisoners. About four miles west of Webbers Falls that Creek boy named Will come riding up in a lather. He had news. He said that morning he was taking some eggs over to Tom Spotted-Gourd and his wife at their place on the Canadian River. When he got there he found the woman out in the yard with the back of her head shot off and the old man inside on the floor with a shotgun wound in his breast.

MR. GOUDY: An objection.

JUDGE PARKER: Confine your testimony to what you saw, Mr. Cogburn.

MR. COGBURN: Yes sir. Well, Deputy Marshal Potter and me rode on down to Spotted-Gourd's place, with the wagon to come on behind us. Deputy Marshal Schmidt stayed

43

with the wagon. When we got to the place we found everything as the boy Will had represented. The woman was out in the yard dead with blowflies on her head and the old man was inside with his breast blowed open by a scatter-gun and his feet burned. He was still alive but he just was. Wind was whistling in and out of the bloody hole. He said about four o'clock that morning them two Wharton boys had rode up there drunk—

MR. GOUDY: An objection.

MR. BARLOW: This is a dying declaration, your honor.

JUDGE PARKER: Overruled. Proceed, Mr. Cogburn.

MR. COGBURN: He said them two Wharton boys, Odus and C. C. by name, had rode up there drunk and throwed down on him with a double barrel shotgun and said, "Tell us where your money is, old man." He would not tell them and they lit some pine knots and held them to his feet and he told them it was in a fruit jar under a gray rock at one corner of the smokehouse. Said he had over four hundred dollars in banknotes in it. Said his wife was crying and taking on all this time and begging for mercy. Said she took off out the door and Odus run to the door and shot her. Said when he raised up off the floor where he was laying Odus turned and shot him. Then they left.

MR. BARLOW: What happened next?

MR. COGBURN: He died on us. Passed away in considerable pain.

MR. BARLOW: Mr. Spotted-Gourd, that is.

MR. COGBURN: Yes sir.

MR. BARLOW: What did you and Marshal Potter do then?

MR. COGBURN: We went out to the smokehouse and that rock had been moved and that jar was gone.

MR. GOUDY: An objection.

JUDGE PARKER: The witness will keep his speculations to himself.

MR. BARLOW: You found a flat gray rock at the corner of the smokehouse with a hollowed-out space under it?

MR. GOUDY: If the prosecutor is going to give evidence I suggest that he be sworn.

JUDGE PARKER: Mr. Barlow, that is not proper examination.

MR. BARLOW: I am sorry, your honor. Marshal Cogburn, what did you find, if anything, at the corner of the smokehouse?

MR. COGBURN: We found a gray rock with a hole right by it.

MR. BARLOW: What was in the hole?

MR. COGBURN: Nothing. No jar or nothing.

MR. BARLOW: What did you do next?

MR. COGBURN: We waited on the wagon to come. When it got there we had a talk amongst ourselves as to who would ride after the Whartons. Potter and me had had dealings with them boys before so we went. It was about a two-hour ride up near where the North Fork strikes the Canadian, on a branch that turns into the Canadian. We got there not long before sundown.

MR. BARLOW: And what did you find?

MR. COGBURN: I had my glass and we spotted the two boys and their old daddy, Aaron Wharton by name, standing down there on the creek bank with some hogs, five or six hogs. They had killed a shoat and was butchering it. It was swinging from a limb and they had built a fire under a wash pot for scalding water. We tied up our horses about a quarter of a mile down the creek and slipped along on foot through the brush so we could get the drop on them. When we showed I told the old man, Aaron Wharton, that we was U.S. marshals and we needed to talk to his boys. He picked up a ax and commenced to cussing us and blackguarding this court.

MR. BARLOW: What did you do?

MR. COGBURN: I started backing away from the ax and tried to talk some sense to him. While this was going on C. C. Wharton edged over by the wash pot behind that steam and picked up a shotgun that was laying up against a saw-log. Potter seen him but it was too late. Before he could get off a shot C. C. Wharton pulled down on him with one barrel and then turned to do the same for me with the other barrel. I shot him and when the old man swung the ax I shot him. Odus lit out for the creek and I shot him. Aaron Wharton and C. C. Wharton was dead when they hit the ground. Odus Wharton was just winged.

MR. BARLOW: Then what happened?

MR. COGBURN: Well, it was all over. I dragged Odus Wharton over to a blackjack tree and cuffed his arms and legs around it with him setting down. I tended to Potter's wound with my handkerchief as best I could. He was in a bad way. I went up to the shack and Aaron Wharton's squaw was there but she would not talk. I searched the premises and found a quart jar under some stove wood that had banknotes in it to the tune of four hundred and twenty dollars.

MR. BARLOW: What happened to Marshal Potter?

MR. COGBURN: He died in this city six days later of septic fever. Leaves a wife and six babies.

MR. GOUDY: An objection.

JUDGE PARKER: Strike the comment.

MR. BARLOW: What became of Odus Wharton?

MR. COGBURN: There he sets.

MR. BARLOW: You may ask, Mr. Goudy.

MR. GOUDY: Thank you, Mr. Barlow. How long did you say you have been a deputy marshal, Mr. Cogburn?

MR. COGBURN: Going on four years.

MR. GOUDY: How many men have you shot in that time?

MR. BARLOW: An objection.

MR. GOUDY: There is more to this shooting than meets the eye, your honor. I am trying to establish the bias of the witness.

JUDGE PARKER: The objection is overruled.

MR. GOUDY: How many, Mr. Cogburn?

MR. COGBURN: I never shot nobody I didn't have to.

MR. GOUDY: That was not the question. How many?

MR. COGBURN: Shot or killed?

MR. GOUDY: Let us restrict it to "killed" so that we may have a manageable figure. How many people have you killed since you became a marshal for this court?

MR. COGBURN: Around twelve or fifteen, stopping men in flight and defending myself.

MR. GOUDY: Around twelve or fifteen. So

many that you cannot keep a precise count. Remember that you are under oath. I have examined the records and a more accurate figure is readily available. Come now, how many?

MR. COGBURN: I believe them two Whartons made twenty-three.

MR. GOUDY: I felt sure it would come to you with a little effort. Now let us see. Twenty-three dead men in four years. That comes to about six men a year.

MR. COGBURN: It is dangerous work.

MR. GOUDY: So it would seem. And yet how much more dangerous for those luckless individuals who find themselves being arrested by you. How many members of this one family, the Wharton family, have you killed?

MR. BARLOW: Your honor, I think counsel should be advised that the marshal is not the defendant in this action.

MR. GOUDY: Your honor, my client and his deceased father and brother were provoked into a gun battle by this man Cogburn. Last spring he shot and killed Aaron Wharton's oldest son and on November second he fairly leaped at the chance to massacre the rest of the family. I will prove that. This assassin Cogburn has too long been clothed with the authority of an honorable court.

The only way I can prove my client's innocence is by bringing out the facts of these two related shootings, together with a searching review of Cogburn's methods. All the other principals, including Marshal Potter, are conveniently dead—

JUDGE PARKER: That will do, Mr. Goudy. Restrain yourself. We shall hear your argument later. The defense will be given every latitude. I do not think the indiscriminate use of such words as "massacre" and "assassin" will bring us any nearer the truth. Pray continue with your cross-examination.

MR. GOUDY: Thank you, your honor. Mr. Cogburn, did you know the late Dub Wharton, brother to the defendant, Odus Wharton?

MR. COGBURN: I had to shoot him in self-defense last April in the Going Snake District of the Cherokee Nation.

MR. GOUDY: How did that come about?

MR. COGBURN: I was trying to serve a warrant on him for selling ardent spirits to the Cherokees. It was not the first one. He come at me with a kingbolt and said, "Rooster, I am going to punch that other eye out." I defended myself.

MR. GOUDY: He was armed with nothing more than a kingbolt from a wagon tongue?

MR. COGBURN: I didn't know what else he had. I saw he had that. I have seen men badly tore up with things no bigger than a kingbolt.

MR. GOUDY: Were you yourself armed?

MR. COGBURN: Yes sir. I had a hand gun.

MR. GOUDY: What kind of hand gun?

MR. COGBURN: A forty-four forty Colt's revolver.

MR. GOUDY: Is it not true that you walked in upon him in the dead of night with that revolver in your hand and gave him no warning?

MR. COGBURN: I had pulled it, yes sir.

MR. GOUDY: Was the weapon loaded and cocked?

MR. COGBURN: Yes sir.

MR. GOUDY: Were you holding it behind you or in any way concealing it?

MR. COGBURN: No sir.

MR. GOUDY: Are you saying that Dub Wharton advanced into the muzzle of that cocked revolver with nothing more than a small piece of iron in his hand?

MR. COGBURN: That was the way of it.

MR. GOUDY: It is passing strange. Now, is it not true that on November second you appeared before Aaron Wharton and his two sons in a similar menacing manner, which is to say, you sprang upon them from cover with that same deadly six-shot revolver in your hand?

MR. COGBURN: I always try to be ready.

MR. GOUDY: The gun was pulled and ready in your hand?

MR. COGBURN: Yes sir.

MR. GOUDY: Loaded and cocked?

MR. COGBURN: If it ain't loaded and cocked it will not shoot.

MR. GOUDY: Just answer my questions if you please.

MR. COGBURN: That one does not make any sense.

JUDGE PARKER: Do not bandy words with counsel, Mr. Cogburn.

MR. COGBURN: Yes sir.

MR. GOUDY: Mr. Cogburn, I now direct your attention back to that scene on the creek bank. It is near dusk. Mr. Aaron Wharton and his two surviving sons are going about their lawful business, secure on their own property. They are butchering a hog so that they might have a little meat for their table—

MR. COGBURN: Them was stolen hogs. That farm belongs to the Wharton squaw, Minnie Wharton.

MR. GOUDY: Your honor, will you instruct this witness to keep silent until he is asked a question?

JUDGE PARKER: Yes, and I will instruct you to start asking questions so that he may respond with answers.

MR. GOUDY: I am sorry, your honor. All right. Mr. Wharton and his sons are on the creek bank. Suddenly, out of the brake, spring two men with revolvers at the ready—

MR. BARLOW: An objection.

JUDGE PARKER: The objection has merit. Mr. Goudy, I have been extremely indulgent. I am going to permit you to continue this line of questioning but I must insist that the cross-examination take the form of questions and answers instead of dramatic soliloquies. And I will caution you that this had best lead to something substantial and fairly soon.

MR. GOUDY: Thank you, your honor. If the court will bear with me for a time. My client has expressed fears about the severity of this court but I have reassured him that no man in this noble Republic loves truth and justice and mercy more than Judge Isaac Parker—

JUDGE PARKER: You are out of order, Mr. Goudy.

MR. GOUDY: Yes sir. All right. Now. Mr. Cogburn, when you and Marshal Potter sprang from the brush, what was Aaron Wharton's reaction on seeing you?

MR. COGBURN: He picked up a ax and commenced to cussing us.

MR. GOUDY: An instinctive reflex against a sudden danger. Was that the nature of the move?

MR. COGBURN: I don't know what that means.

MR. GOUDY: You would not have made such a move yourself?

MR. COGBURN: If it was me and Potter with the drop I would have done what I was told.

MR. GOUDY: Yes, exactly, you and Potter. We can agree that the Whartons were in peril of their lives. All right. Let us go back to yet an earlier scene, at the Spotted-Gourd home, around the wagon. Who was in charge of that wagon?

MR. COGBURN: Deputy Marshal Schmidt.

MR. GOUDY: He did not want you to go to the Wharton place, did he?

MR. COGBURN: We talked about it some and he agreed Potter and me should go.

MR. GOUDY: But at first he did not want you to go, did he, knowing there was bad blood between you and the Whartons?

MR. COGBURN: He must have wanted me to go or he would not have sent me.

MR. GOUDY: You had to persuade him, did you not?

MR. COGBURN: I knowed the Whartons and I

was afraid somebody would get killed going up against them.

MR. GOUDY: As it turned out, how many were killed?

MR. COGBURN: Three. But the Whartons did not get away. It could have been worse.

MR. GOUDY: Yes, you might have been killed yourself.

MR. COGBURN: You mistake my meaning. Three murdering thieves might have got loose and gone to kill somebody else. But you are right that I might have been killed myself. It was mighty close at that and it is no light matter to me.

MR. GOUDY: Nor to me. You are truly one of nature's survivors, Mr. Cogburn, and I do not make light of your gift. I believe you testified that you backed away from Aaron Wharton.

MR. COGBURN: That is right.

MR. GOUDY: You were backing away?

MR. COGBURN: Yes sir. He had that ax raised.

MR. GOUDY: Which direction were you going?

MR. COGBURN: I always go backwards when I am backing up.

MR. GOUDY: I appreciate the humor of that remark. Aaron Wharton was standing by the wash pot when you arrived?

MR. COGBURN: It was more like squatting. He was stoking up the fire under the pot.

MR. GOUDY: And where was the ax?

MR. COGBURN: Right there at his hand.

MR. GOUDY: Now you say you had a cocked revolver clearly visible in your hand and yet he picked up that ax and advanced upon you, somewhat in the manner of Dub Wharton with that nail or rolled-up paper or whatever it was in his hand?

MR. COGBURN: Yes sir. Commenced to cussing and laying about with threats.

MR. GOUDY: And you were backing away? You were moving away from the direction of the wash pot?

MR. COGBURN: Yes sir.

MR. GOUDY: How far did you back up before the shooting started?

MR. COGBURN: About seven or eight steps.

MR. GOUDY: Meaning Aaron Wharton advanced on you about the same distance, some seven or eight steps?

MR. COGBURN: Something like that.

MR. GOUDY: What would that be? About sixteen feet?

MR. COGBURN: Something like that.

MR. GOUDY: Will you explain to the jury why his body was found immediately by the wash pot with one arm in the fire, his sleeve and hand smoldering?

MR. COGBURN: I don't think that is where he was.

MR. GOUDY: Did you move the body after you had shot him?

MR. COGBURN: No sir.

MR. GOUDY: You did not drag his body back to the fire?

MR. COGBURN: No sir. I don't think that is where he was.

MR. GOUDY: Two witnesses who arrived on the scene moments after the shooting will testify to the location of the body. You don't remember moving the body?

MR. COGBURN: If that is where he was I might have moved him. I don't remember it.

MR. GOUDY: Why did you place the upper part of his body in the fire?

MR. COGBURN: Well, I didn't do it.

MR. GOUDY: Then you did not move him and he was not advancing upon you at all. Or you did move him and throw his body in the flames. Which? Make up your mind.

MR. COGBURN: Them hogs that was rooting around there might have moved him.

MR. GOUDY: Hogs indeed.

JUDGE PARKER: Mr. Goudy, darkness is upon us. Do you think you can finish with this witness in the next few minutes?

MR. GOUDY: I will need more time, your honor.

JUDGE PARKER: Very well. You may resume at eight-thirty o'clock tomorrow morning.

Mr. Cogburn, you will return to the witness stand at that time. The jury will not talk to others or converse amongst themselves about this case. The defendant is remanded to custody.

The judge rapped his gavel and I jumped, not looking for that noise. The crowd broke up to leave. I had not been able to get a good look at that Odus Wharton but now I did when he stood up with an officer on each side of him. Even though he had one arm in a sling they kept his wrists cuffed in court. That was how dangerous he was. If there ever was a man with black murder in his countenance it was Odus Wharton. He was a half-breed with eyes that were mean and close-set and that stayed open all the time like snake eyes. It was a face hardened in sin. Creeks are good Indians, they say, but a Creek-white like him or a Creek-Negro is something else again.

When the officers were taking Wharton out he passed by Rooster Cogburn and said something to him, some ugly insult or threat, you could tell. Rooster just looked at him. The people pushed me on through the door and outside. I waited on the porch.

Rooster was one of the last ones out. He had a paper in one hand and a sack of tobacco in the other and he was trying to roll a cigarette. His hands were shaking and he was spilling tobacco.

I approached him and said, "Mr. Rooster Cogburn?"

He said, "What is it?" His mind was on something else.

I said, "I would like to talk with you a minute."

He looked me over. "What is it?" he said.

I said, "They tell me you are a man with true grit."

He said, "What do you want, girl? Speak up. It is suppertime."

I said, "Let me show you how to do that." I took the half-made cigarette and shaped it up and licked it and sealed it and twisted the ends and gave it back to him. It was pretty loose because he had already wrinkled the paper. He lit it and it flamed up and burned about halfway down.

I said, "Your makings are too dry."

He studied it and said, "Something."

I said, "I am looking for the man who shot and killed my father, Frank Ross, in front of the Monarch boardinghouse. The man's name is Tom Chaney. They say he is over in the Indian Territory and I need somebody to go after him."

He said, "What is your name, girl? Where do you live?"

"My name is Mattie Ross," I replied. "We are located in Yell County near Dardanelle. My mother is at home looking after my sister Victoria and my brother Little Frank."

"You had best go home to them," said he. "They will need some help with the churning."

I said, "The high sheriff and a man in the marshal's office have given me the full particulars. You can get a fugitive warrant for Tom Chaney and go after him. The Government will pay you two dollars for bringing him in plus ten cents a mile for each of you. On top of that I will pay you a fifty-dollar reward."

"You have looked into this a right smart," said he.

"Yes, I have," said I. "I mean business."

He said, "What have you got there in your poke?"

I opened the sugar sack and showed him.

"By God!" said he. "A Colt's dragoon! Why, you are no bigger than a corn nubbin! What are you doing with that pistol?"

I said, "It belonged to my father. I intend to kill Tom Chaney with it if the law fails to do so."

"Well, that piece will do the job. If you can find a high stump to rest it on while you take aim and shoot."

"Nobody here knew my father and I am afraid nothing much is going to be done about Chaney except I do it myself. My brother is a child and my mother's people are in Monterey, California. My Grandfather Ross is not able to ride."

"I don't believe you have fifty dollars."

"I will have it in a day or two. Have you heard of a robber called Lucky Ned Pepper?"

"I know him well. I shot him in the lip last August down in the Winding Stair Mountains. He was plenty lucky that day."

"They think Tom Chaney has tied up with him."

"I don't believe you have fifty dollars, baby sister, but if you are hungry I will give you supper and we will talk it over and make medicine. How does that suit you?"

I said it suited me right down to ground. I figured he would live in a house with his family and was not prepared to discover that he had only a small room in the back of a Chinese grocery store on a dark street. He did not have a wife. The Chinaman was called Lee. He had a supper ready of boiled potatoes and stew meat. The three of us ate at a low table with a coal-oil lamp in the middle of it. There was a blanket for a tablecloth. A little bell rang once and Lee went up front through a curtain to wait on a customer.

Rooster said he had heard about the shooting of my father but did not know the details. I told him. I noticed by the lamplight that his bad left eye was not completely shut. A little crescent of white showed at the bottom and glistened in the light. He ate with a spoon in one hand and a wadded-up piece of white bread in the other, with considerable sopping. What a contrast to the Chinaman with his delicate chopsticks! I had never seen them in use before. Such nimble fingers! When the coffee had boiled Lee got the pot off the stove and started to pour. I put my hand over my cup.

"I do not drink coffee, thank you."

Rooster said, "What do you drink?"

"I am partial to cold buttermilk when I can get it."

"Well, we don't have none," said he. "Nor lemonade either."

"Do you have any sweet milk?"

Lee went up front to his icebox and brought back a jar of milk. The cream had been skimmed from it.

I said, "This tastes like blue-john to me."

Rooster took my cup and put it on the floor and a fat brindle cat appeared out of the darkness where the bunks were and came over to lap up the milk. Rooster said, "The General is not so hard to please." The cat's name was General Sterling Price. Lee served some honey cakes for dessert and Rooster spread butter and preserves all over his like a small child. He had a "sweet tooth."

I offered to clean things up and they took me at my word. The pump and the washstand were outside. The cat followed me out for the scraps. I did the best I could on the enamelware plates with a rag and yellow soap and cold water. When I got back inside Rooster and Lee were playing cards on the table.

Rooster said, "Let me have my cup." I gave it to him and he poured some whiskey in it from a demijohn. Lee smoked a long pipe.

I said, "What about my proposition?"

Rooster said, "I am thinking on it."

"What is that you are playing?"

"Seven-up. Do you want a hand?"

"I don't know how to play it. I know how to play bid whist."

"We don't play bid whist."

I said, "It sounds like a mighty easy way to make fifty dollars to me. You would just be doing your job anyway, and getting extra pay besides."

"Don't crowd me," said he. "I am thinking about expenses."

I watched them and kept quiet except for blowing my nose now and again. After a time I said, "I don't see how you can play cards and drink whiskey and think about this detective business all at the same time."

He said, "If I'm going up against Ned Pepper I will need a hundred dollars. I have figured out that much. I will want fifty dollars in advance."

"You are trying to take advantage of me."

"I am giving you my children's rate," he said. "It will not be a easy job of work, smoking Ned out. He will be holed up down there in the hills in the Choctaw Nation. There will be expenses."

"I hope you don't think I am going to keep you in whiskey."

"I don't have to buy that, I confiscate it. You might try a little touch of it for your cold."

"No, thank you."

"This is the real article. It is double-rectified bust-head from Madison County, aged in the keg. A little spoonful would do you a power of good."

"I would not put a thief in my mouth to steal my brains."

"Oh, you wouldn't, would you?"

"No, I wouldn't."

"Well, a hundred dollars is my price, sis. There it is."

"For that kind of money I would want a guarantee. I would want to be pretty sure of what I was getting."

"I have not yet seen the color of your money."

"I will have the money in a day or two. I will think about your proposition and talk to you again. Now I want to go to the Monarch boardinghouse. You had better walk over there with me."

"Are you scared of the dark?"

"I never was scared of the dark."

"If I had a big horse pistol like yours I would not be scared of any booger-man."

"I am not scared of the booger-man. I don't know the way over there."

"You are a lot of trouble. Wait until I finish this hand. You cannot tell what a Chinaman is thinking. That is how they beat you at cards."

They were betting money on the play and Rooster was not winning. I kept after him but he would only say, "One more hand," and pretty soon I was asleep with my head on the table. Some time later he began to shake me.

"Wake up," he was saying. "Wake up, baby sister."

"What is it?" said I.

He was drunk and he was fooling around with Papa's pistol. He pointed out something on the floor over by the curtain that opened into the store. I looked and it was a big long barn rat. He sat there hunkered on the floor, his tail flat, and he was eating meal that was spilling out of a hole in the sack. I gave a start but Rooster put his tobacco-smelling hand over my mouth and gripped my cheeks and held me down.

He said, "Be right still." I looked around for Lee and figured he must have gone to bed. Rooster said, "I will try this the new way. Now watch." He leaned forward and spoke at the rat in a low voice, saying, "I have a writ here that says for you to stop eating Chen Lee's corn meal forthwith. It is a rat writ. It is a writ for a rat and this is lawful service of said writ." Then he looked over at me and said, "Has he stopped?" I gave no reply. I have never wasted any time encouraging drunkards or show-offs. He said, "It don't look like to me he has stopped." He was holding Papa's revolver down at his left side and he fired twice without aiming. The noise filled up that little room and made the curtains jump. My ears rang. There was a good deal of smoke.

Lee sat up in his bunk and said, "Outside is place for shooting."

"I was serving some papers," said Rooster.

The rat was a mess. I went over and picked him up by the tail and pitched him out the back door for

Sterling, who should have smelled him out and dispatched him in the first place.

I said to Rooster, "Don't be shooting that pistol again. I don't have any more loads for it."

He said, "You would not know how to load it if you did have."

"I know how to load it."

He went to his bunk and pulled out a tin box that was underneath and brought it to the table. The box was full of oily rags and loose cartridges and odd bits of leather and string. He brought out some lead balls and little copper percussion caps and a tin of powder.

He said, "All right, let me see you do it. There is powder, caps and bullets."

"I don't want to right now. I am sleepy and I want to go to my quarters at the Monarch boardinghouse."

"Well, I didn't think you could," said he.

He commenced to reload the two chambers. He dropped things and got them all askew and did not do a good job. When he had finished he said, "This piece is too big and clumsy for you. You are better off with something that uses cartridges."

He poked around in the bottom of the box and came up with a funny little pistol with several barrels. "Now this is what you need," he said. "It is a twenty-two pepper-box that shoots five times, and sometimes all at once. It is called 'The Ladies' Companion.' There is a sporting lady called Big

Faye in this city who was shot twice with it by her stepsister. Big Faye dresses out at about two hundred and ninety pounds. The bullets could not make it through to any vitals. That was unusual. It will give you good service against ordinary people. It is like new. I will trade you even for this old piece."

I said, "No, that was Papa's gun. I am ready to go. Do you hear me?" I took my revolver from him and put it back in the sack. He poured some more whiskey in his cup.

"You can't serve papers on a rat, baby sister."

"I never said you could."

"These shitepoke lawyers think you can but you can't. All you can do with a rat is kill him or let him be. They don't care nothing about papers. What is your thinking on it?"

"Are you going to drink all that?"

"Judge Parker knows. He is a old carpetbagger but he knows his rats. We had a good court here till the pettifogging lawyers moved in on it. You might think Polk Goudy is a fine gentleman to look at his clothes, but he is the sorriest son of a bitch that God ever let breathe. I know him well. Now they have got the judge down on me, and the marshal too. The rat-catcher is too hard on the rats. That is what they say. *Let up on them rats! Give them rats a fair show!* What kind of show did they give Columbus Potter? Tell me that. A finer man never lived."

I got up and walked out thinking I would shame him into coming along and seeing that I got home all right but he did not follow. He was still talking when I left. The town was quite dark at that end and I walked fast and saw not a soul although I heard music and voices and saw lights up toward the river where the barrooms were.

When I reached Garrison Avenue I stopped and got my bearings. I have always had a good head for directions. It did not take me long to reach the Monarch. The house was dark. I went around to the back door with the idea that it would be unlocked because of the toilet traffic. I was right. Since I had not yet paid for another day it occurred to me that Mrs. Floyd might have installed a new guest in Grandma Turner's bed, perhaps some teamster or railroad detective. I was much relieved to find my side of the bed vacant. I got the extra blankets and arranged them as I had done the night before. I said my prayers and it was some time before I got any sleep. I had a cough.

I WAS SICK the next day. I got up and went to breakfast but I could not eat much and my eyes and nose were running so I went back to bed. I felt very low. Mrs. Floyd wrapped a rag around my neck that was soaked in turpentine and smeared with lard. She dosed me with something called Dr. Underwood's Bile Activator. "You will pass blue water for a day or two but do not be alarmed as that is only the medicine working," she said. "It will relax you wonderfully. Grandma Turner and I bless the day we discovered it." The label on the bottle said it did not contain mercury and was commended by physicians and clergymen.

Along with the startling color effect the potion also caused me to be giddy and lightheaded. I suspect now that it made use of some such ingredient as codeine or laudanum. I can remember when half the old ladies in the country were "dopeheads."

Thank God for the Harrison Narcotics Law. Also the Volstead Act. I know Governor Smith is "wet" but that is because of his race and religion and he is not personally accountable for that. I think his first loyalty is to his country and not to "the infallible Pope of Rome." I am not afraid of Al Smith for a minute. He is a good Democrat and when he is elected I believe he will do the right thing if he is not hamstrung by the Republican gang and bullied into an early grave as was done to Woodrow Wilson, the greatest Presbyterian gentleman of the age.

I stayed in bed for two days. Mrs. Floyd was kind and brought my meals to me. The room was so cold that she did not linger to ask many questions. She inquired twice daily at the post office for my letter.

Grandma Turner got in the bed each afternoon for her rest and I would read to her. She loved her medicine and would drink it from a water glass. I read her about the Wharton trial in the *New Era* and the *Elevator*. I also read a little book someone had left on the table called *Bess Calloway's Disappointment*. It was about a girl in England who could not make up her mind whether to marry a rich man with a pack of dogs named Alec or a preacher. She was a pretty girl in easy circumstances who did not have to cook or work at anything and she could have either one she wanted. She made trouble for herself because she would never say what she meant but only blush and talk around it. She kept everybody in a stir wondering what she was driving at. That was what held your interest. Grandma Turner and I both enjoyed it. I had to read the humorous parts twice. Bess married one of the two beaus and he turned out to be mean and thoughtless. I forget which one it was.

On the evening of the second day I felt a little better and I got up and went to supper. The drummer was gone with his midget calculators and there were four or five other vacancies at the table as well.

Toward the end of the meal a stranger came in wearing two revolvers and made known that he was seeking room and board. He was a nice-looking man around thirty years of age with a "cowlick" at the crown of his head. He needed a bath and a shave but you could tell that was not his usual condition. He looked to be a man of good family. He had pale-blue eyes and auburn hair. He was wearing a long corduroy coat. His manner was stuck-up and he had a smug grin that made you nervous when he turned it on you.

He forgot to take off his spurs before sitting down at the table and Mrs. Floyd chided him, saying she did not want her chair legs scratched up any more than they were, which was considerable. He apologized and complied with her wish. The spurs were the Mexican kind with big rowels. He put them up on the table by his plate. Then he remembered his revolvers and he unbuckled the gun belt and hung it on the back of his chair. This was a fancy rig. The belt was thick and wide and bedecked with cartridges and the handles on his pistols were white. It was like something you might see today in a "Wild West" show.

His grin and his confident manner cowed

71

everybody at the table but me and they stopped talking and made a to-do about passing him things, like he was somebody. I must own too that he made me worry a little about my straggly hair and red nose.

While he was helping himself to the food he grinned at me across the table and said, "Hidy."

I nodded and said nothing.

"What is your name?" said he.

"Pudding and tame," said I.

He said, "I will take a guess and say it is Mattie Ross."

"How do you know that?"

"My name is LaBoeuf," he said. He called it La-Beef but spelled it something like LaBoeuf. "I saw your mother just two days ago. She is worried about you."

"What was your business with her, Mr. LaBoeuf?"

"I will disclose that after I eat. I would like to have a confidential conversation with you."

"Is she all right? Is anything wrong?"

"No, she is fine. There is nothing wrong. I am looking for someone. We will talk about it after supper. I am very hungry."

Mrs. Floyd said, "If it is something touching on her father's death we know all about that. He was murdered in front of this very house. There is still blood on my porch where they carried his body."

The man LaBoeuf said, "It is about something else."

Mrs. Floyd described the shooting again and tried to draw him out on his business but he only smiled and went on eating and would not be drawn.

After supper we went to the parlor, to a corner away from the other borders, and LaBoeuf set up two chairs there facing the wall. When we were seated in this curious arrangement he took a small photograph from his corduroy coat and showed it to me. The picture was wrinkled and dim. I studied it. The face of the man was younger and there was no black mark but there was no question but it was the likeness of Tom Chaney. I told LaBoeuf as much.

He said, "Your mother has also identified him. Now I will give you some news. His real name is Theron Chelmsford. He shot and killed a state senator named Bibbs down in Waco, Texas, and I have been on his trail the best part of four months. He dallied in Monroe, Louisiana, and Pine Bluff, Arkansas, before turning up at your father's place."

I said, "Why did you not catch him in Monroe, Louisiana, or Pine Bluff, Arkansas?"

"He is a crafty one."

"I thought him slow-witted myself."

"That was his act."

"It was a good one. Are you some kind of law?"

LaBoeuf showed me a letter that identified him as a Sergeant of Texas Rangers, working out of a place called Ysleta near El Paso. He said, "I am on detached service just now. I am working for the family of Senator Bibbs in Waco."

"How came Chaney to shoot a senator?"

"It was about a dog. Chelmsford shot the senator's bird dog. Bibbs threatened to whip him over it and Chelmsford shot the old gentleman while he was sitting in a porch swing."

"Why did he shoot the dog?"

"I don't know that. Just meanness. Chelmsford is a hard case. He claims the dog barked at him. I don't know if he did or not."

"I am looking for him too," said I, "this man you call Chelmsford."

"Yes, that is my understanding. I had a conversation with the sheriff today. He informed me that you were staying here and looking for a special detective to go after Chelmsford in the Indian Territory."

"I have found a man for the job."

"Who is the man?"

"His name is Cogburn. He is a deputy marshal for the Federal Court. He is the toughest one they have and he is familiar with a band of robbers led by Lucky Ned Pepper. They believe Chaney has tied up with that crowd."

"Yes, that is the thing to do," said LaBoeuf. "You need a Federal man. I am thinking along those lines myself. I need someone who knows the ground and can make an arrest out there that will stand up. You cannot tell what the courts will do these days. I might get Chelmsford all the way down to McLennan County, Texas, only to have some corrupt judge say he was kidnapped and turn him loose. Wouldn't that be something?"

"It would be a letdown."

"Maybe I will throw in with you and your marshal."

"You will have to talk to Rooster Cogburn about that."

"It will be to our mutual advantage. He knows the land and I know Chelmsford. It is at least a two-man job to take him alive."

"Well, it is nothing to me one way or the other except that when we do get Chaney he is not going to Texas, he is coming back to Fort Smith and hang."

"Haw haw," said LaBoeuf. "It is not important where he hangs, is it?"

"It is to me. Is it to you?"

"It means a good deal of money to me. Would not a hanging in Texas serve as well as a hanging in Arkansas?"

"No. You said yourself they might turn him loose down there. This judge will do his duty."

"If they don't hang him we will shoot him. I can give you my word as a Ranger on that."

"I want Chaney to pay for killing my father and not some Texas bird dog."

"It will not be for the dog, it will be for the

senator, and your father too. He will be just as dead that way, you see, and pay for all his crimes at once."

"No, I do not see. That is not the way I look at it."

"I will have a conversation with the marshal."

"It's no use talking to him. He is working for me. He must do as I say."

"I believe I will have a conversation with him all the same."

I realized I had made a mistake by opening up to this stranger. I would have been more on my guard had he been ugly instead of nice-looking. Also my mind was soft and not right from being doped by the bile activator.

I said, "You will not have a conversation with him for a few days at any rate."

"How is that?"

"He has gone to Little Rock."

"On what business?"

"Marshal business."

"Then I will have a conversation with him when he returns."

"You will be wiser to get yourself another marshal. They have aplenty of them. I have already made an arrangement with Rooster Cogburn."

"I will look into it," said he. "I think your mother would not approve of your getting mixed up in this kind of enterprise. She thinks you are seeing about a horse. Criminal investigation is sordid and dangerous and is best left in the hands of men who know the work."

"I suppose that is you. Well, if in four months I could not find Tom Chaney with a mark on his face like banished Cain I would not undertake to advise others how to do it."

"A saucy manner does not go down with me."

"I will not be bullied."

He stood up and said, "Earlier tonight I gave some thought to stealing a kiss from you, though you are very young, and sick and unattractive to boot, but now I am of a mind to give you five or six good licks with my belt."

"One would be as unpleasant as the other," I replied. "Put a hand on me and you will answer for it. You are from Texas and ignorant of our ways but the good people of Arkansas do not go easy on men who abuse women and children."

"The youth of Texas are brought up to be polite and to show respect for their elders."

"I notice people of that state also gouge their horses with great brutal spurs."

"You will push that saucy line too far."

"I have no regard for you."

He was angered and thus he left me, clanking away in all his Texas trappings.

I ROSE EARLY the next morning, somewhat improved though still wobbly on my feet. I dressed quickly and made haste to the post office without waiting for breakfast. The mail had come in but it was still being sorted and the delivery window was not yet open.

I gave a shout through the slot where you post letters and brought a clerk to the window. I identified myself and told him I was expecting a letter of an important legal nature. He knew of it through Mrs. Floyd's inquiries and he was good enough to interrupt his regular duties to search it out. He found it in a matter of minutes.

I tore it open with impatient fingers. There it was, the notarized release (money in my pocket!), and a letter from Lawyer Daggett as well.

The letter ran thus:

My Dear Mattie:

I trust you will find the enclosed document satisfactory. I wish you would leave these matters entirely to me or, at the very least, do me the courtesy of consulting me before making such agreements. I am not scolding you but I am saying that your headstrong ways will lead you into a tight corner one day.

That said, I shall concede that you seem to

have driven a fair bargain with the good colonel. I know nothing of the man, of his probity or lack of same, but I should not give him this release until I had the money in hand. I feel sure you have taken his measure.

Your mother is bearing up well but is much concerned for you and anxious for your speedy return. I join her in that. Fort Smith is no place for a young girl alone, not even a "Mattie." Little Frank is down with an earache but of course that is no serious matter. Victoria is in fine fettle. It was thought best that she not attend the funeral.

Mr. MacDonald is still away on his deer hunt and Mr. Hardy was pressed into service to preach Frank's funeral, taking his text from the 16th chapter of John, "I have overcome the world." I know Mr. Hardy is not much esteemed for his social qualities but he is a good man in his way and no one can say he is not a diligent student of the Scriptures. The Danville lodge had charge of the graveside service. Needless to say, the whole community is shocked and grieved. Frank was a rich man in friends.

Your mother and I shall expect you to take the first train home when you have concluded your business with the colonel. You will wire me immediately with regard to that and we shall look for you in a day or two. I should like to get Frank's estate through probate without delay and there are important matters to be discussed with you. Your mother will make no decision without you, nor will she sign anything, not even common receipts; hence nothing can move forward until you are here. You are her strong right arm now, Mattie, and you are a pearl of great price to me, but there are times when you are an almighty trial to those who love you. Hurry home! I am

Thine Truly,
Jno. Daggett

If you want anything done right you will have to see to it yourself every time. I do not know to this day why they let a wool-hatted crank like Owen Hardy preach the service. Knowing the Gospel and preaching it are two different things. A Baptist or even a Campbellite would have been better than him. If I had been home I would never have permitted it but I could not be in two places at once.

Stonehill was not in a quarrelsome mood that morning, indeed he was not snorting or blowing at all but rather in a sad, baffled state like that of some elderly lunatics I have known. Let me say quickly that the man was not crazy. My comparison is not a kind one and I would not use it except to emphasize his changed manner.

He wanted to write me a check and I know that

it would have been all right but I did not wish to take the affair this far and risk being rooked, so I insisted on cash money. He said he would have it as soon as his bank opened.

I said, "You do not look well."

He said, "My malaria is making its annual visitation."

"I have been a little under the weather myself. Have you taken any quinine?"

"Yes, I am stuffed to the gills with the Peruvian bark. My ears are fairly ringing from it. It does not take hold as it once did."

"I hope you will be feeling better."

"Thank you. It will pass."

I returned to the Monarch to get the breakfast I had paid for. LaBoeuf the Texan was at the table, shaved and clean. I supposed he could do nothing with the "cowlick." It is likely that he cultivated it. He was a vain and cocky devil. Mrs. Floyd asked me if the letter had come.

I said, "Yes, I have the letter. It came this morning."

"Then I know you are relieved," said she. Then to the others, "She has been awaiting that letter for days." Then back to me, "Have you seen the colonel yet?"

"I have just now come from that place," I replied.

LaBoeuf said, "What colonel is that?"

"Why, Colonel Stockhill the stone trader," said Mrs. Floyd.

I broke in to say, "It is a personal matter."

"Did you get your settlement?" said Mrs. Floyd, who could no more keep her mouth closed than can a yellow catfish.

"What kind of stones?" said LaBoeuf.

"It is Stonehill the stock trader," said I. "He does not deal in stones but livestock. I sold him some half-starved ponies that came up from Texas. There is nothing more to it."

"You are powerful young for a horsetrader," said LaBoeuf. "Not to mention your sex."

"Yes, and you are powerful free for a stranger," said I.

"Her father bought the ponies from the colonel just before he was killed," said Mrs. Floyd. "Little Mattie here stood him down and made him take them back at a good price."

Right around nine o'clock I went to the stock barn and exchanged my release for three hundred and twenty-five dollars in greenbacks. I had held longer amounts in my hand but this money, I fancied, would be pleasing out of proportion to its face value. But no, it was only three hundred and twenty-five dollars in paper and the moment fell short of my expectations. I noted the mild disappointment and made no more of it than that. Perhaps I was affected by Stonehill's downcast state.

I said, "Well, you have kept your end of the agreement and I have kept mine."

"That is so," said he. "I have paid you for a horse I do not possess and I have bought back a string of useless ponies I cannot sell again."

"You are forgetting the gray horse."

"Crow bait."

"You are looking at the thing in the wrong light."

"I am looking at it in the light of God's eternal truth."

"I hope you do not think I have wronged you in any way."

"No, not at all," said he. "My fortunes have been remarkably consistent since I came to the 'Bear State.' This is but another episode, and a relatively happy one. I was told this city was to be the Chicago of the Southwest. Well, my little friend, it is not the Chicago of the Southwest. I cannot rightly say what it is. I would gladly take pen in hand and write a thick book on my misadventures here, but dare not for fear of being called a lying romancer."

"The malaria is making you feel bad. You will soon find a buyer for the ponies."

"I have a tentative offer of ten dollars per head from the Pfitzer Soap Works of Little Rock."

"It would be a shame to destroy such spirited horseflesh and render it into soap."

"So it would. I am confident the deal will fall through."

"I will return later for my saddle."

"Very good."

83

I went to the Chinaman's store and bought an apple and asked Lee if Rooster was in. He said he was still in bed. I had never seen anyone in bed at ten o'clock in the morning who was not sick but that was where he was.

He stirred as I came through the curtain. His weight was such that the bunk was bowed in the middle almost to the floor. It looked like he was in a hammock. He was fully clothed under the covers. The brindle cat Sterling Price was curled up on the foot of the bed. Rooster coughed and spit on the floor and rolled a cigarette and lit it and coughed some more. He asked me to bring him some coffee and I got a cup and took the eureka pot from the stove and did this. As he drank, little brown drops of coffee clung to his mustache like dew. Men will live like billy goats if they are let alone. He seemed in no way surprised to see me so I took the same line and stood with my back to the stove and ate my apple.

I said, "You need some more slats in that bed."

"I know," said he. "That is the trouble, there is no slats in it at all. It is some kind of a damned Chinese rope bed. I would love to burn it up."

"It is not good for your back sleeping like that."

"You are right about that too. A man my age ought to have a good bed if he has nothing else. How does the weather stand out there?"

"The wind is right sharp," said I. "It is clouding up some in the east."

"We are in for snow or I miss my guess. Did you see the moon last night?"

"I do not look for snow today."

"Where have you been, baby sister? I looked for you to come back, then give up on you. I figured you went on home."

"No, I have been at the Monarch boardinghouse right along. I have been down with something very nearly like the croup."

"Have you now? The General and me will thank you not to pass it on."

"I have about got it whipped. I thought you might inquire about me or look in on me while I was laid up."

"What made you think that?"

"I had no reason except I did not know anybody else in town."

"Maybe you thought I was a preacher that goes around paying calls on all the sick people."

"No, I did not think that."

"Preachers don't have nothing better to do. I had my work to see to. Your Government marshals don't have time to be paying a lot of social calls. They are too busy trying to follow all the regulations laid down by Uncle Sam. That gentleman will have his fee sheets just and correct or he does not pay."

"Yes, I see they are keeping you busy."

"What you see is a honest man who has worked half the night on his fee sheets. It is the devil's own work and Potter is not here to help me. If you don't have no schooling you are up against it in this country, sis. That is the way of it. No sir, that man has no chance any more. No matter if he has got sand in his craw, others will push him aside, little thin fellows that have won spelling bees back home."

I said, "I read in the paper where they are going to hang the Wharton man."

"There was nothing else they could do," said he. "It is too bad they cannot hang him three or four times."

"When will they do the job?"

"It is set for January but Lawyer Goudy is going to Washington city to see if President Hayes will not commute the sentence. The boy's mother, Minnie Wharton, has got some property and Goudy will not let up till he has got it all."

"Will the President let him off, do you think?"

"It is hard to say. What does the President know about it? I will tell you. Nothing. Goudy will claim the boy was provoked and he will tell a bushel of lies about me. I should have put a ball in that boy's head instead of his collarbone. I was thinking about my fee. You will sometimes let money interfere with your notion of what is right."

I took the folded currency from my pocket and held it up, showing it to him.

Rooster said, "By God! Look at it! How much

have you got there? If I had your hand I would throw mine in."

"You did not believe I would come back, did you?"

"Well, I didn't know. You are a hard one to figure."

"Are you still game?"

"Game? I was born game, sis, and hope to die in that condition."

"How long will it take you to get ready to go?"

"Ready to go where?"

"To the Territory. To the Indian Territory to get Tom Chaney, the man who shot my father, Frank Ross, in front of the Monarch boardinghouse."

"I forget just what our agreement was."

"I offered to pay you fifty dollars for the job."

"Yes, I remember that now. What did I say to that?"

"You said your price was a hundred dollars."

"That's right, I remember now. Well, that's what it still is. It will take a hundred dollars."

"All right."

"Count it out there on the table."

"First I will have an understanding. Can we leave for the Territory this afternoon?"

He sat up in the bed. "Wait," he said. "Hold up. You are not going."

"That is part of it," said I.

"It cannot be done."

"And why not? You have misjudged me if you

think I am silly enough to give you a hundred dollars and watch you ride away. No, I will see the thing done myself."

"I am a bonded U.S. marshal."

"That weighs but little with me. R. B. Hayes is the U.S. President and they say he stole Tilden out."

"You never said anything about this. I cannot go up against Ned Pepper's band and try to look after a baby at one and the same time."

"I am not a baby. You will not have to worry about me."

"You will slow me down and get in my way. If you want this job done and done fast you will let me do it my own way. Credit me for knowing my business. What if you get sick again? I can do nothing for you. First you thought I was a preacher and now you think I am a doctor with a flat stick who will look at your tongue every few minutes."

"I will not slow you down. I am a good enough rider."

"I will not be stopping at boardinghouses with warm beds and plates of hot grub on the table. It will be traveling fast and eating light. What little sleeping is done will take place on the ground."

"I have slept out at night. Papa took me and Little Frank coon hunting last summer on the Petit Jean."

"Coon hunting?"

"We were out in the woods all night. We sat around a big fire and Yarnell told ghost stories. We had a good time."

"Blast coon hunting! This ain't no coon hunt, it don't come in forty miles of being a coon hunt!"

"It is the same idea as a coon hunt. You are just trying to make your work sound harder than it is."

"Forget coon hunting. I am telling you that where I am going is no place for a shirttail kid."

"That is what they said about coon hunting. Also Fort Smith. Yet here I am."

"The first night out you will be taking on and crying for your mama."

I said, "I have left off crying, and giggling as well. Now make up your mind. I don't care anything for all this talk. You told me what your price for the job was and I have come up with it. Here is the money. I aim to get Tom Chaney and if you are not game I will find somebody who *is* game. All I have heard out of you so far is talk. I know you can drink whiskey and I have seen you kill a gray rat. All the rest has been talk. They told me you had grit and that is why I came to you. I am not paying for talk. I can get all the talk I need and more at the Monarch boardinghouse."

"I ought to slap your face."

"How do you propose to do it from that hog wallow you are sunk in? I would be ashamed of myself living in this filth. If I smelled as bad as you I would not live in a city, I would go live on top of Magazine Mountain where I would offend no one but rabbits and salamanders."

He came up out of the bunk and spilt his coffee and sent the cat squalling. He reached for me but I moved quickly out of his grasp and got behind the stove. I picked up a handful of expense sheets from the table and jerked up a stove lid with a lifter. I held them over the flames. "You had best stand back if these papers have any value to you," said I.

He said, "Put them sheets back on the table."

I said, "Not until you stand back."

He moved back a step or two. "That is not far enough," said I. "Go back to the bed."

Lee looked in through the curtain. Rooster sat down on the edge of the bed. I put the lid back on the stove and returned the papers to the table.

"Get back to your store," said Rooster, turning his anger on Lee. "Everything is all right. Sis and me is making medicine."

I said, "All right, what have you to say? I am in a hurry."

He said, "I cannot leave town until them fee sheets is done. Done and accepted."

I sat down at the table and worked over the sheets for better than an hour. There was nothing hard about it, only I had to rub out most of what he had already done. The forms were ruled with places for the entries and figures but Rooster's handwriting was so large and misguided that it covered the lines and wandered up and down into places where it should not have gone. As a consequence the written entries did not always match up with the money figures.

What he called his "vouchers" were scribbled notes, mostly undated. They ran such as this: "Rations for Cecil $1.25," and "Important words with Red .65 cts."

"Red who?" I inquired. "They are not going to pay for this kind of thing."

"That is Society Red," said he. "He used to cut cross-ties for the Katy. Put it down anyway. They might pay a little something on it."

"When was it? What was it for? How could you pay sixty-five cents for important words?"

"It must have been back in the summer. He ain't been seen since August when he tipped us on Ned that time."

"Was that what you paid him for?"

"No, Schmidt paid him off on that. I reckon it was cartridges I give him. I give a lot of cartridges away. I cannot recollect every little transaction."

"I will date it August fifteenth."

"We can't do that. Make it the seventeenth of October. Everything on this bunch has to come after the first of October. They won't pay behind that. We will date all the old ones ahead a little bit."

"You said you haven't seen the man since August."

"Let us change the name to Pig Satterfield and

91

make the date the seventeenth of October. Pig helps us on timber cases and them clerks is used to seeing his name."

"His Christian name is Pig?"

"I never heard him called anything else."

I pressed him for approximate dates and bits of fact that would lend substance to the claims. He was very happy with my work. When I was finished he admired the sheets and said, "Look how neat they are. Potter never done a job like this. They will go straight through or I miss my bet."

I wrote out a short agreement regarding the business between us and had him sign it. I gave him twenty-five dollars and told him I would give him another twenty-five when we made our departure. The fifty dollars balance would be paid on the successful completion of the job.

I said, "That advance money will cover the expenses for the both of us. I expect you to provide the food for us and the grain for our horses."

"You will have to bring your own bedding," said he.

"I have blankets and a good oilskin slicker. I will be ready to go this afternoon as soon as I have got me a horse."

"No," said he, "I will be tied up at the Courthouse. There are things I must attend to. We can get off at first light tomorrow. We will cross the ferry for I must pay a call on an informer in the Cherokee Nation."

"I will see you later today and make final plans."

I took dinner at the Monarch. The man LaBoeuf did not appear and I hopefully assumed he had moved on for some distant point. After a brief nap I went to the stock barn and looked over the ponies in the corral. There did not seem to be a great deal of difference in them, apart from color, and at length I decided on a black one with white forelegs.

He was a pretty thing. Papa would not own a horse with more than one white leg. There is a foolish verse quoted by horsemen to the effect that such a mount is no good, and particularly one with four white legs. I forget just how the verse goes but you will see later that there is nothing in it.

I found Stonehill in his office. He was wrapped in a shawl and sitting very close to his stove and holding his hands up before it. No doubt he was suffering from a malarial chill. I pulled up a box and sat down beside him and warmed myself.

He said, "I just received word that a young girl fell head first into a fifty-foot well on the Towson Road. I thought perhaps it was you."

"No, it was not I."

"She was drowned, they say."

"I am not surprised."

"Drowned like the fair Ophelia. Of course with her it was doubly tragic. She was distracted from a broken heart and would do nothing to save herself. I am amazed that people can bear up and carry on under these repeated blows. There is no end to them."

"She must have been silly. What do you hear from the Little Rock soap man?"

"Nothing. The matter is still hanging fire. Why do you ask?"

"I will take one of those ponies off your hands. The black one with the white stockings in front. I will call him 'Little Blackie.' I want him shod this afternoon."

"What is your offer?"

"I will pay the market price. I believe you said the soap man offered ten dollars a head."

"That is a lot price. You will recall that I paid you twenty dollars a head only this morning."

"That was the market price at that time."

"I see. Tell me this, do you entertain plans of ever leaving this city?"

"I am off early tomorrow for the Choctaw Nation. Marshal Rooster Cogburn and I are going after the murderer Chaney."

"Cogburn?" said he. "How did you light on that greasy vagabond?"

"They say he has grit," said I. "I wanted a man with grit."

"Yes, I suppose he has that. He is a notorious thumper. He is not a man I should care to share a bed with."

"No more would I."

"Report has it that he rode by the light of the

moon with Quantrill and Bloody Bill Anderson. I would not trust him too much. I have heard too that he was *particeps criminis* in some road-agent work before he came here and attached himself to the Courthouse."

"He is to be paid when the job is done," said I. "I have given him a token payment for expenses and he is to receive the balance when we have taken our man. I am paying a good fee of one hundred dollars."

"Yes, a splendid inducement. Well, perhaps it will all work out to your satisfaction. I shall pray that you return safely, your efforts crowned with success. It may prove to be a hard journey."

"The good Christian does not flinch from difficulties."

"Neither does he rashly court them. The good Christian is not willful or presumptuous."

"You think I am wrong."

"I think you are wrongheaded."

"We will see."

"Yes, I am afraid so."

Stonehill sold me the pony for eighteen dollars. The Negro smith caught him and brought him inside on a halter and filed his hoofs and nailed shoes on him. I brushed the burrs away and rubbed him down. He was frisky and spirited but not hysterical and he submitted to the treatment without biting or kicking us.

I put a bridle on him but I could not lift Papa's

saddle easily and I had the smith saddle him. He offered to ride the pony first. I said I thought I could handle him. I climbed gingerly aboard. Little Blackie did nothing for a minute or so and then he took me by surprise and pitched twice, coming down hard with his forelegs stiff, giving severe jolts to my "tailbone" and neck. I would have been tossed to the ground had I not grabbed the saddle horn and a handful of mane. I could get a purchase on nothing else, the stirrups being far below my feet. The smith laughed but I was little concerned with good form or appearance. I rubbed Blackie's neck and talked softly to him. He did not pitch again but neither would he move forward.

"He don't know what to make of a rider so light as you," said the smith. "He thinks they is a horsefly on his back."

He took hold of the reins near the pony's mouth and coaxed him to walk. He led him around inside the big barn for a few minutes, then opened one of the doors and took him outside. I feared the daylight and cold wind would set Blackie off anew, but no, I had made me a "pal."

The smith let go of the reins and I rode the pony down the muddy street at a walk. He was not very responsive to the reins and he worried his head around over the bit. It took me a while to get him turned around. He had been ridden before but not, I gathered, in a good long time. He soon fell into it. I rode him about town until he was lightly sweating.

When I got back to the barn the smith said, "He ain't so mean, is he?"

I said, "No, he is a fine pony."

I adjusted the stirrups up as high as they would go and the smith unsaddled Little Blackie and put him in a stall. I fed him some corn but only a small measured amount as I was afraid he might founder himself on the rich grain. Stonehill had been feeding the ponies largely on hay.

It was growing late in the day. I hurried over to Lee's store, very proud of my horse and full of excitement at the prospect of tomorrow's adventure. My neck was sore from being snapped but that was a small enough bother, considering the enterprise that was afoot.

I went in the back door without knocking and found Rooster sitting at the table with the man LaBoeuf. I had forgotten about him.

"What are you doing here?" said I.

"Hidy," said LaBoeuf. "I am having a conversation with the marshal. He did not go to Little Rock after all. It is a business conversation."

Rooster was eating candy. He said, "Set down, sis, and have a piece of taffy. This jaybird calls himself LaBoeuf. He claims he is a State Ranger in Texas. He come up here to tell us how the cow eat the cabbage."

I said, "I know who he is."

"He says he is on the track of our man. He wants to throw in with us."

"I know what he wants and I have already told him we are not interested in his help. He has gone behind my back."

"What is it?" said Rooster. "What is the trouble?"

"There is no trouble, except of his own making," said I. "He made a proposition and I turned it down. That is all. We don't need him."

"Well now, he might come in handy," said Rooster. "It will not cost us anything. He has a big-bore Sharps carbine if we are jumped by buffaloes or elephants. He says he knows how to use it. I say let him go. We might run into some lively work."

"No, we don't need him," said I. "I have already told him that. I have got my horse and everything is ready. Have you seen to all your business?"

Rooster said, "Everything is ready but the grub and it is working. The chief deputy wanted to know who had done them sheets. He said he would put you on down there at good wages if you want a job. Potter's wife is fixing the eats. She is not what I call a good cook but she is good enough and she needs the money."

LaBoeuf said, "I reckon I must have the wrong man. Do you let little girls hooraw you, Cogburn?"

Rooster turned his cold right eye on the Texan. "Did you say hooraw?"

"Hooraw," said LaBoeuf. "That was the word."

"Maybe you would like to see some real hoorawing."

"There is no hoorawing in it," said I. "The marshal is working for me. I am paying him."

"How much are you paying him?" asked LaBoeuf.

"That is none of your affair."

"How much is she paying you, Cogburn?"

"She is paying enough," said Rooster.

"Is she paying five hundred dollars?"

"No."

"That is what the Governor of Texas has put up for Chelmsford."

"You don't say so," said Rooster. He thought it over. Then he said, "Well, it sounds good but I have tried to collect bounties from states and railroads too. They will lie to you quicker than a man will. You do good to get half what they say they will pay. Sometimes you get nothing. Anyhow, it sounds queer. Five hundred dollars is mightly little for a man that killed a senator."

"Bibbs was a little senator," said LaBoeuf. "They would not have put up anything except it would look bad."

"What is the terms?" said Rooster.

"Payment on conviction."

Rooster thought that one over. He said, "We might have to kill him."

"Not if we are careful."

"Even if we don't they might not convict him," said Rooster. "And even if they do, by the time they do there will be a half dozen claims for the money from little top-water peace officers down there. I believe I will stick with sis."

"You have not heard the best part," said LaBoeuf.

"The Bibbs family has put up fifteen hundred dollars for Chelmsford."

"Have they now?" said Rooster. "The same terms?"

"No, the terms are these: just deliver Chelmsford up to the sheriff of McLennan County, Texas. They don't care if he is alive or dead. They pay off as soon as he is identified."

"That is more to my liking," said Rooster. "How do you figure on sharing the money?"

LaBoeuf said, "If we take him alive I will split that fifteen hundred dollars down the middle with you and claim the state reward for myself. If we have to kill him I will give you a third of the Bibbs money. That is five hundred dollars."

"You mean to keep all the state money yourself?"

"I have put in almost four months on this job. I think it is owing to me."

"Will the family pay off?"

LaBoeuf replied, "I will be frank to say the Bibbses are not loose with their money. It holds to them like the cholera to a nigger. But I guess they will have to pay. They have made public statements and run notices in the paper. There is a son, Fatty Bibbs, who wants to run for the man's seat in Austin. He will be obliged to pay."

He took the reward notices and newspaper cuttings out of his corduroy coat and spread them out on the table. Rooster looked them over for some little time. He said, "Tell me what your objection is, sis. Do you wish to cut me out of some extra money?"

I said, "This man wants to take Chaney back to Texas. That is not what I want. That was not our agreement."

Rooster said, "We will be getting him all the same. What you want is to have him caught and punished. We still mean to do that."

"I want him to know he is being punished for killing my father. It is nothing to me how many dogs and fat men he killed in Texas."

"You can let him know that," said Rooster. "You can tell him to his face. You can spit on him and make him eat sand out of the road. You can put a ball in his foot and I will hold him while you do it. But we must catch him first. We will need some help. You are being stiff-necked about this. You are young. It is time you learned that you cannot have your way in every little particular. Other people have got their interests too."

"When I have bought and paid for something I will have my way. Why do you think I am paying you if not to have my way?"

LaBoeuf said, "She is not going anyhow. I don't

understand this conversation. It is not sensible. I am not used to consulting children in my business. Run along home, little britches, your mama wants you."

"Run home yourself," said I. "Nobody asked you to come up here wearing your big spurs."

"I told her she could go," said Rooster. "I will see after her."

"No," said LaBoeuf. "She will be in the way."

Rooster said, "You are taking a lot on yourself."

LaBoeuf said, "She will spell nothing but trouble and confusion. You know that as well as I do. Stop and think. She has got you buffaloed with her saucy ways."

Rooster said, "Maybe I will just catch this Chaney myself and take all the money."

LaBoeuf considered it. "You might deliver him," he said. "I would see you did not collect anything for it."

"How would you do that, jaybird?"

"I would dispute your claim. I would muddy the waters. They will not want much to back down. When it is all over they might shake your hand and thank you for your trouble and they might not."

"If you did that I would kill you," said Rooster. "Where is your profit?"

"Where is yours?" said LaBoeuf. "And I would not count too much on being able to shade somebody I didn't know."

"I can shade you all right," said Rooster. "I never seen anybody from Texas I couldn't shade. Get crossways of me, LaBoeuf, and you will think a thousand of brick has fell on you. You will wisht you had been at the Alamo with Travis."

"Knock him down, Rooster," said I.

LaBoeuf laughed. He said, "I believe she is trying to hooraw you again. Look here, I have had enough quarreling. Let us get on with our business. You have done your best to accommodate this little lady, more than most people would do, and yet she will still be contrary. Send her on her way. We will get her man. That is what you agreed to do. What if something happens to her? Have you thought about that? Her people will blame you and maybe the law will have something to say too. Why don't you think about yourself? Do you think she is concerned with your interest? She is using you. You have got to be firm."

Rooster said, "I would hate to see anything happen to her."

"You are thinking about that reward money," said I. "It is a pig in a poke. All you have heard from LaBoeuf is talk and I have paid you cash money. If you believe anything he says I do not credit you with much sense. Look at him grin. He will cheat you."

Rooster said, "I must think about myself some too, sis."

I said, "Well, what are you going to do? You cannot carry water on both shoulders."

"We will get your man," said he. "That is the main thing."

"Let me have my twenty-five dollars. Hand it over."

"I have spent it all."

"You sorry piece of trash!"

"I will try and get it back to you. I will send it to you."

"That's a big story! If you think you are going to cheat me like this you are mistaken! You have not seen the last of Mattie Ross, not by a good deal!"

I was so mad I could have bitten my tongue off. Sterling Price the cat sensed my mood and he tucked his ears back and scampered from my path, giving me a wide berth.

I suppose I must have cried a little but it was a cold night and by the time I reached the Monarch my anger had cooled to the point where I could think straight and lay plans. There was not time enough to get another detective. Lawyer Daggett would be up here soon looking for me, probably no later than tomorrow. I thought about making a complaint to the head marshal. No, there was time for that later. I would have Lawyer Daggett skin Rooster Cogburn and nail his verminous hide to the wall. The important thing was not to lose sight of my object and that was to get Tom Chaney.

I took supper and then set about getting my things together. I had Mrs. Floyd prepare some bacon and biscuits and make little sandwiches of them. But not so little as all that, as one of her biscuits would have made two of Mama's. Very flat though, she skimped on baking powder. I also bought a small wedge of cheese from her and some dried peaches. These things I secured in a sack.

Mrs. Floyd was alive with curiosity and I told her I was going over into the Territory with some marshals to look at a man they had arrested. This did not satisfy her by any means but I pleaded ignorance of details. I told her I would likely be gone for several days and if my mother or Lawyer Daggett made inquiries (a certainty) she was to reassure them as to my safety.

I rolled up the blankets with the sack of food inside and then wrapped the slicker around the roll and made it fast with some twine. I put Papa's heavy coat on over my own coat. I had to turn the cuffs back. My little hat was not as thick and warm as his so I traded. Of course it was too big and I had to fold up some pages from the *New Era* and stick them inside the band to make for a snug fit. I took my bundle and my gun sack and left for the stock barn.

Stonehill was just leaving when I got there. He was singing the hymn *Beulah Land* to himself in a low bass voice. It is one of my favorites. He stopped singing when he saw me.

"It is you again," said he. "Is there some complaint about the pony?"

"No, I am very happy with him," said I. "Little Blackie is my 'chum.' "

"A satisfied customer gladdens the heart."

"I believe you have picked up some since last I saw you."

"Yes, I am a little better. Richard's himself again. Or will be ere the week is out. Are you leaving us?"

"I am getting an early start tomorrow and I thought I would stay the balance of the night in your barn. I don't see why I should pay Mrs. Floyd a full rate for only a few hours' sleep."

"Why indeed."

He took me inside the barn and told the watchman it would be all right for me to stay the night on the office bunk. The watchman was an old man. He helped me to shake out the dusty quilt that was on the bunk. I looked in on Little Blackie at his stall and made sure everything was in readiness. The watchman followed me around.

I said to him, "Are you the one that had his teeth knocked out?"

"No, that was Tim. Mine was drawn by a dentist. He called himself a dentist."

"Who are you?"

"Toby."

"I want you to do something."

"What are you up to?"

"I am not free to discuss it. Here is a dime for you. At two hours before sunup I want you to feed this pony. Give him a double handful of oats and about the same amount of corn, but no more, along with a little hay. See that he has sufficient water. At one hour before sunup I want you to wake me up. When you have done that, put this saddle and this bridle on the pony. Have you got it all straight?"

"I am not simple, I am just old. I have handled horses for fifty years."

"Then you should do a good job. Do you have any business in the office tonight?"

"I cannot think of any."

"If you do have, take care of it now."

"There is nothing I need in there."

"That's fine. I will close the door and I do not want a lot of coming and going while I am trying to sleep."

I slept well enough wrapped in the quilt. The fire in the office stove had been banked but the little room was not so cold as to be very uncomfortable. The watchman Toby was true to his word and he woke me in the chill darkness before dawn. I was up and buttoning my boots in a moment. While Toby saddled the horse I washed myself, using some of his hot coffee water to take the sting out of a bucket of cold water.

It came to me that I should have left one of the bacon sandwiches out of the bundle for breakfast, but you can never think of everything. I did not want to open it up now. Toby gave me a portion of his grits that he had warmed up.

"Do you not have any butter to put on it?" I asked him.

"No," said he, and I had to eat it plain. I tied my roll behind the saddle as I had seen Papa do and I made doubly sure it was secure.

I could see no good place to carry the pistol. I wanted the piece ready at hand but the belt was too big around for my waist and the pistol itself was far too big and heavy to stick in the waist of my jeans. I finally tied the neck of the gun sack to the saddle horn with a good knot about the size of a turkey egg.

I led Little Blackie from his stall and mounted him. He was a little nervous and jumpy but he did not pitch. Toby tightened the girth again after I was aboard.

He said, "Have you got everything?"

"Yes, I believe I am ready. Open the door, Toby, and wish me luck. I am off for the Choctaw Nation."

It was still dark outside and bitter cold although mercifully there was little wind. Why is it calm in the early morning? You will notice that lakes are usually still and smooth before daybreak. The frozen, rutted mud of the streets made uncertain going for Little Blackie in his new shoes. He snorted and snapped his head from time to time as though to look at me. I talked to him, saying silly things.

Only four or five people were to be seen as I rode down Garrison Avenue, and they scurrying from one warm place to another. I could see lamps coming on through windows as the good people of Fort Smith began to stir for the new day.

When I reached the ferry slip on the river I dismounted and waited. I had to move and dance about to keep from getting stiff. I removed the paper wadding from inside the hatband and pulled the hat down over my ears. I had no gloves and I rolled Papa's coat sleeves down so that my hands might be covered.

There were two men running the ferry. When it reached my side and discharged a horseman, one of the ferrymen hailed me.

"Air you going acrost?" said he.

"I am waiting for someone," said I. "What is the fare?"

"Ten cents for a horse and rider."

"Have you seen Marshal Cogburn this morning?"

"Is that Rooster Cogburn?"

"That is the man."

"We have not seen him."

There were few passengers at that hour but as soon as one or two turned up the ferry would depart. It seemed to have no schedule except as business demanded, but then the crossing was not a long one. As gray dawn came I could make out chunks of ice bobbing along out in the current of the river.

The boat made at least two circuits before Rooster and LaBoeuf appeared and came riding down the incline to the slip. I had begun to worry that I might have missed them. Rooster was mounted on a big bay stallion that stood at about sixteen hands, and LaBoeuf on a shaggy cow pony not much bigger than mine.

Well, they were a sight to see with all their arms. They were both wearing their belt guns around their outside coats and LaBoeuf cut a splendid figure with his white-handled pistols and Mexican spurs. Rooster was wearing a deerskin jacket over his black suit coat. He carried only one revolver on his belt, an ordinary-looking piece with grips of cedar or some reddish wood. On the other side, the right side, he wore a dirk knife. His gun belt was not fancy like LaBoeuf's but only a plain and narrow belt with no cartridge loops. He carried his cartridges in a sack in his pocket. But he also had two more revolvers in saddle scabbards at his thighs. They were big pistols like mine. The two officers also packed saddle guns, Rooster a Winchester repeating rifle and LaBoeuf a gun called a Sharps rifle, a kind I had never seen. My thought was this: *Chaney, look out!*

They dismounted and led their horses aboard the ferry in a clatter and I followed at a short distance. I said nothing. I was not trying to hide but neither did I do anything to call attention to myself. It was a minute or so before Rooster recognized me.

"Sure enough, we have got company," said he.

LaBoeuf was very angry. "Can you not get anything through your head?" he said to me. "Get off this boat. Did you suppose you were going with us?"

I replied, "This ferry is open to the public. I have paid my fare."

LaBoeuf reached in his pocket and brought out a gold dollar. He handed it to one of the ferrymen and said, "Slim, take this girl to town and present her to the sheriff. She is a runaway. Her people are worried nearly to death about her. There is a fifty-dollar reward for her return."

"That is a story," said I.

"Let us ask the marshal," said LaBoeuf. "What about it, marshal?"

Rooster said, "Yes, you had best take her away. She is a runaway all right. Her name is Ross and she came up from Yell County. The sheriff has a notice on her."

"They are in this story together," said I. "I have business across the river and if you interfere with me, Slim, you may find yourself in court where you don't want to be. I have a good lawyer."

But the tall river rat would pay no heed to my protests. He led my pony back on to the slip and the boat pulled away without me. I said, "I am not going to walk up the hill." I mounted Little Blackie and the river rat led us up the hill. When we reached the top I said, "Wait, stop a minute." He said, "What is it?" I said, "There is something wrong with my hat." He stopped and turned around. "Your hat?" said he. I took it off and slapped him in the face with it two or three times and made him drop the reins. I recovered them and wheeled Little Blackie about and rode him down the bank for all he was worth. I had no spurs or switch but I used my hat on his flank to good effect.

About fifty yards below the ferry slip the river narrowed and I aimed for the place, going like blazes across a sandbar. I popped Blackie all the way with my hat as I was afraid he might shy at the water and I did not want to give him a chance to think about it. We hit the river running and Blackie snorted and arched his back against the icy water, but once he was in he swam as though he was raised to it. I drew up my legs behind me and held to the saddle horn and gave Blackie his head with loose reins. I was considerably splashed.

The crossing was badly chosen because the narrow place of a river is the deepest and it is there that the current is swiftest and the banks steepest, but these things did not occur to me at the time; shortest looked best. We came out some little ways down the river and, as I say, the bank was steep and Blackie had some trouble climbing it.

When we were up and free I reined in and Little Blackie gave himself a good shaking. Rooster and LaBoeuf and the ferryman were looking at us from the boat. We had beaten them across. I stayed where I was. When they got off the boat LaBoeuf hailed me, saying, "Go back, I say!" I made no reply. He and Rooster had a parley.

Their game soon became clear. They mounted quickly and rode off at a gallop with the idea of leaving me. What a foolish plan, pitting horses so heavily loaded with men and hardware against a pony so lightly burdened as Blackie!

Our course was northwesterly on the Fort Gibson Road, if you could call it a road. This was the Cherokee Nation. Little Blackie had a hard gait, a painful trot, and I made him speed up and slow down until he had achieved a pace, a kind of lope, that was not so jarring. He was a fine, spirited pony. He enjoyed this outing, you could tell.

We rode that way for two miles or more, Blackie and I hanging back from the officers at about a hundred yards. Rooster and LaBoeuf at last saw that they were making no gain and they slowed their horses to a walk. I did the same. After a mile or so of this they stopped and dismounted. I stopped too, keeping my distance, and remained in the saddle.

LaBoeuf shouted, "Come here! We will have a conversation with you!"

"You can talk from there!" I replied. "What is it you have to say?"

The two officers had another parley.

Then LaBoeuf shouted to me again, saying, "If you do not go back now I am going to whip you!"

I made no reply.

LaBoeuf picked up a rock and threw it in my direction. It fell short by about fifty yards.

I said, "That is the most foolish thing that ever I saw!"

LaBoeuf said, "Is that what you will have, a whipping?"

I said, "You are not going to whip anybody!"

They talked some more between themselves but could not seem to settle on anything and after a time they rode off again, this time at a comfortable lope.

Few travelers were on the road, only an Indian now and then on a horse or a mule, or a family in a spring wagon. I will own I was somewhat afraid of them although they were not, as you may imagine, wild Comanches with painted faces and outlandish garb but rather civilized Creeks and Cherokees and Choctaws from Mississippi and Alabama who had owned slaves and fought for the Confederacy and wore store clothes. Neither were they sullen and grave. I thought them on the cheerful side as they nodded and spoke greetings.

From time to time I would lose sight of Rooster and LaBoeuf as they went over a rise or around a bend of trees, but only briefly. I had no fears that they could escape me.

Now I will say something about the land. Some people think the present state of Oklahoma is all treeless plains. They are wrong. The eastern part (where we were traveling) is hilly and fairly well timbered with post oak and blackjack and similar hard scrub. A little farther south there is a good deal of pine as well, but right along in here at this time of year the only touches of green to be seen were cedar brakes and solitary holly trees and a few big cypresses down in the bottoms. Still, there were open places, little meadows and prairies, and from the tops of those low hills you could usually see a good long distance.

Then this happened. I was riding along woolgathering instead of keeping alert and as I came over a rise I discovered the road below me deserted. I nudged the willing Blackie with my heels. The two officers could not be far ahead. I knew they were up to some "stunt."

At the bottom of the hill there was a stand of trees and a shallow creek. I was not looking for them there at all. I thought they had raced on ahead. Just as Blackie was splashing across the creek Rooster and LaBoeuf sprang from the brush on their horses. They were right in my path. Little Blackie reared and I was almost thrown.

LaBoeuf was off his horse before you could say "Jack Robinson," and at my side. He pulled me from the saddle and threw me to the ground, face down. He twisted one of my arms behind me and put his knee in my back. I kicked and struggled but the big Texan was too much for me.

"Now we will see what tune you sing," said he. He snapped a limb off a willow bush and commenced to push one of my trouser legs above my boot. I kicked violently so that he could not manage the trouser leg.

Rooster remained on his horse. He sat up there in the saddle and rolled a cigarette and watched. The more I kicked the harder LaBoeuf pressed down with his knee and I soon saw the game was up. I left off struggling. LaBoeuf gave me a couple of sharp licks with the switch. He said, "I am going to stripe your leg good."

"See what good it does you!" said I. I began to cry, I could not help it, but more from anger and embarrassment than pain. I said to Rooster, "Are you going to let him do this?"

He dropped his cigarette to the ground and said, "No, I don't believe I will. Put your switch away, LaBoeuf. She has got the best of us."

"She has not got the best of me," replied the Ranger.

Rooster said, "That will do, I said."

LaBoeuf paid him no heed.

Rooster raised his voice and said, "Put that switch down, LaBoeuf! Do you hear me talking to you?"

LaBoeuf stopped and looked at him. Then he said, "I am going ahead with what I started."

Rooster pulled his cedar-handled revolver and cocked it with his thumb and threw down on

LaBoeuf. He said, "It will be the biggest mistake you ever made, you Texas brush-popper."

LaBoeuf flung the switch away in disgust and stood up. He said, "You have taken her part in this all along, Cogburn. Well, you are not doing her any kindness here. Do you think you are doing the right thing? I can tell you you are doing the wrong thing."

Rooster said, "That will do. Get on your horse."

I brushed the dirt from my clothes and washed my hands and face in the cold creek water. Little Blackie was getting himself a drink from the stream. I said, "Listen here, I have thought of something. This 'stunt' that you two pulled has given me an idea. When we locate Chaney a good plan will be for us to jump him from the brush and hit him on the head with sticks and knock him insensible. Then we can bind his hands and feet with rope and take him back alive. What do you think?"

But Rooster was angry and he only said, "Get on your horse."

We resumed our journey in thoughtful silence, the three of us now riding together and pushing deeper into the Territory to I knew not what.

DINNERTIME came and went and on we rode. I was hungry and aching but I kept my peace for I knew the both of them were waiting for me to complain or say something that would make me out a "tenderfoot." I was determined not to give them anything to chaff me about. Some large wet flakes of snow began to fall, then changed to soft drizzling rain, then stopped altogether, and the sun came out. We turned left off the Fort Gibson Road and headed south, back down toward the Arkansas River. I say "down." South is not "down" any more than north is "up." I have seen maps carried by emigrants going to California that showed west at the top and east at the bottom.

Our stopping place was a store on the riverbank. Behind it there was a small ferry boat.

We dismounted and tied up our horses. My legs were tingling and weak and I tottered a little as I walked. Nothing can take the starch out of you like a long ride on horseback.

A black mule was tied up to the porch of the store. He had a cotton rope around his neck right under his jaw. The sun had caused the wet rope to draw up tight and the mule was gasping and choking for breath. The more he tugged the worse he made it. Two wicked boys were sitting on the edge of the porch laughing at the mule's discomfort. One was white and the other was an Indian. They were about seventeen years of age.

Rooster cut the rope with his dirk knife and the mule breathed easy again. The grateful beast wandered off shaking his head about. A cypress stump served for a step up to the porch. Rooster went up first and walked over to the two boys and kicked them off into the mud with the flat at his boot. "Call that sport, do you?" said he. They were two mighty surprised boys.

The storekeeper was a man named Bagby with an Indian wife. They had already had dinner but the woman warmed up some catfish for us that she had left over. LaBoeuf and I sat at a table near the stove and ate while Rooster had a conference with the man Bagby at the back of the store.

The Indian woman spoke good English and I learned to my surprise that she too was a Presbyterian. She had been schooled by a missionary. What preachers we had in those days! Truly they took the word into "the highways and hedges." Mrs. Bagby was not a Cumberland Presbyterian but a member of the U.S. or Southern Presbyterian Church. I too am now a member of the Southern Church. I say nothing against the Cumberlands. They broke with the Presbyterian Church because they did not believe a preacher needed a lot of formal education. That is all right but they are not sound on Election. They do not fully accept it. I confess it is a hard doctrine, running contrary to our earthly ideas of fair play, but I can see no way around it. Read I Corinthians 6:13 and II Timothy 1:9, 10. Also I Peter 1:2, 19, 20 and Romans 11:7. There you have it. It was good for Paul and Silas and it is good enough for me. It is good enough for you too.

Rooster finished his parley and joined us in our fish dinner. Mrs. Bagby wrapped up some gingerbread for me to take along. When we went back out on the porch Rooster kicked the two boys into the mud again.

He said, "Where is Virgil?"

The white boy said, "He and Mr. Simmons is off down in the bottoms looking for strays."

"Who is running the ferry?"

"Me and Johnny."

"You don't look like you have sense enough to run a boat. Either one of you."

"We know how to run it."

"Then let us get to it."

"Mr. Simmons will want to know who cut his mule loose," said the boy.

"Tell him it was Mr. James, a bank examiner of Clay County, Missouri," said Rooster. "Can you remember the name?"

"Yes sir."

We led our horses down to the water's edge. The boat or raft was a rickety, waterlogged affair and the horses nickered and balked when we tried to make them go aboard. I did not much blame them.

LaBoeuf had to blindfold his shaggy pony. There just was room for all of us.

Before casting off, the white boy said, "You said James?"

"That is the name," said Rooster.

"The James boys are said to be slight men."

"One of them has grown fat," said Rooster.

"I don't believe you are Jesse or Frank James either one."

"The mule will not range far," said Rooster. "See that you mend your ways, boy, or I will come back some dark night and cut off your head and let the crows peck your eyeballs out. Now you and Admiral Semmes get us across this river and be damned quick about it."

A ghostly fog lay on top of the water and it enveloped us, about to the waist of a man, as we pushed off. Mean and backward though they were, the two boys handled the boat with considerable art. They pulled and guided us along on a heavy rope that was tied fast to trees on either bank. We swung across in a looping downstream curve with the current doing most of the work. We got our feet wet and I was happy to get off the thing.

The road we picked up on the south bank was little more than a pig trail. The brush arched over and closed in on us at the top and we were slapped and stung with limbs. I was riding last and I believe I got the worst of it.

Here is what Rooster learned from the man

Bagby: Lucky Ned Pepper had been seen three days earlier at McAlester's store on the M. K. & T. Railroad tracks. His intentions were not known. He went there from time to time to pay attention to a lewd woman. A robber called Haze and a Mexican had been seen in his company. And that was all the man knew.

Rooster said we would be better off if we could catch the robber band before they left the neighborhood of McAlester's and returned to their hiding place in the fastness of the Winding Stair Mountains.

LaBoeuf said, "How far is it to McAlester's?"

"A good sixty miles," said Rooster. "We will make another fifteen miles today and get an early start tomorrow."

I groaned and made a face at the thought of riding another fifteen miles that day and Rooster turned and caught me. "How do you like this coon hunt?" said he.

"Do not be looking around for me," said I. "I will be right here."

LaBoeuf said, "But Chelmsford was not with him?"

Rooster said, "He was not seen at McAlester's with him. It is certain he was with him on the mail hack job. He will be around somewhere near or I miss my guess. The way Ned cuts his winnings I know the boy did not realize enough on that job to travel far."

We made a camp that night on the crest of a hill where the ground was not so soggy. It was a very dark night. The clouds were low and heavy and neither the moon or stars could be seen. Rooster gave me a canvas bucket and sent me down the hill about two hundred yards for water. I carried my gun along. I had no lantern and I stumbled and fell with the first bucket before I got far and had to retrace my steps and get another. LaBoeuf unsaddled the horses and fed them from nosebags. On the second trip I had to stop and rest about three times coming up the hill. I was stiff and tired and sore. I had the gun in one hand but it was not enough to balance the weight of the heavy bucket which pulled me sideways as I walked.

Rooster was squatting down building a fire and he watched me. He said, "You look like a hog on ice."

I said, "I am not going down there again. If you want any more water you will have to fetch it yourself."

"Everyone in my party must do his job."

"Anyhow, it tastes like iron."

LaBoeuf was rubbing down his shaggy pony. He said, "You are lucky to be traveling in a place where a spring is so handy. In my country you can ride for days and see no ground water. I have lapped filthy water from a hoofprint and was glad to have it. You don't know what discomfort is until you have nearly perished for water."

Rooster said, "If I ever meet one of you Texas waddies that says he never drank from a horse track I think I will shake his hand and give him a Daniel Webster cigar."

"Then you don't believe it?" asked LaBoeuf.

"I believed it the first twenty-five times I heard it."

"Maybe he did drink from one," said I. "He is a Texas Ranger."

"Is that what he is?" said Rooster. "Well now, I can believe that."

LaBoeuf said, "You are getting ready to show your ignorance now, Cogburn. I don't mind a little personal chaffing but I won't hear anything against the Ranger troop from a man like you."

"The Ranger troop!" said Rooster, with some contempt. "I tell you what you do. You go tell John Wesley Hardin about the Ranger troop. Don't tell me and sis."

"Anyhow, we know what we are about. That is more than I can say for you political marshals."

Rooster said, "How long have you boys been mounted on sheep down there?"

LaBoeuf stopped rubbing his shaggy pony. He said, "This horse will be galloping when that big American stud of yours is winded and collapsed. You cannot judge by looks. The most villainous-looking pony is often your gamest performer. What would you guess this pony cost me?"

Rooster said, "If there is anything in what you say I would guess about a thousand dollars."

"You will have your joke, but he cost me a hundred and ten dollars," said LaBoeuf. "I would not sell him for that. It is hard to get in the Rangers if you do not own a hundred-dollar horse."

Rooster set about preparing our supper. Here is what he brought along for "grub": a sack of salt and a sack of red pepper and a sack of taffy—all this in his jacket pockets—and then some ground coffee beans and a big slab of salt pork and one hundred and seventy corn dodgers. I could scarcely credit it. The "corn dodgers" were balls of what I would call hot-water cornbread. Rooster said the woman who prepared them thought the order was for a wagon party of marshals.

"Well," said he, "when they get too hard to eat plain we can make mush from them and what we have left we can give to the stock."

He made some coffee in a can and fried some pork. Then he sliced up some of the dodgers and fried the pieces in grease. Fried bread! That was a new dish to me. He and LaBoeuf made fast work of about a pound of pork and a dozen dodgers. I ate some of my bacon sandwiches and a piece of gingerbread and drank the rusty-tasting water. We had a blazing fire and the wet wood crackled fiercely and sent off showers of sparks. It was cheerful and heartening against the gloomy night.

LaBoeuf said he was not accustomed to such a big fire, that in Texas they frequently had little more than a fire of twigs or buffalo chips with which to warm up their beans. He asked Rooster if it was wise to make our presence known in unsettled country with a big fire. He said it was Ranger policy not to sleep in the same place as where they had cooked their supper. Rooster said nothing and threw more limbs on the fire.

I said, "Would you two like to hear the story of 'The Midnight Caller'? One of you will have to be 'The Caller.' I will tell you what to say. I will do all the other parts myself."

But they were not interested in hearing ghost stories and I put my slicker on the ground as close to the fire as I dared and proceeded to make my bed with the blankets. My feet were so swollen from the ride that my boots were hard to pull off. Rooster and LaBoeuf drank some whiskey but it did not make them sociable and they sat there without talking. Soon they got out their bed rolls.

Rooster had a nice buffalo robe for a ground sheet. It looked warm and comfortable and I envied him for it. He took a horsehair lariat from his saddle and arranged it in a loop around his bed.

LaBoeuf watched him and grinned. He said, "That is a piece of foolishness. All the snakes are asleep this time of year."

"They have been known to wake up," said Rooster.

I said, "Let me have a rope too. I am not fond of snakes."

"A snake would not bother with you," said Rooster. "You are too little and bony."

He put an oak log in the fire and banked coals and ashes against it and turned in for the night. Both the officers snored and one of them made a wet mouth noise along with it. It was disgusting. Exhausted as I was, I had trouble falling asleep. I was warm enough but there were roots and rocks under me and I moved this way and that trying to improve my situation. I was sore and the movement was painful. I finally despaired of ever getting fixed right. I said my prayers but did not mention my discomfort. This trip was my own doing.

When I awoke there were snowflakes on my eyes. Big moist flakes were sifting down through the trees. There was a light covering of white on the ground. It was not quite daylight but Rooster was already up, boiling coffee and frying meat. LaBoeuf was attending to the horses and he had them saddled. I wanted some hot food so I passed up the biscuits and ate some of the salt meat and fried bread. I shared my cheese with the officers. My hands and face smelled of smoke.

Rooster hurried us along in breaking camp. He was concerned about the snow. "If this keeps up we will want shelter tonight," he said. LaBoeuf had already fed the stock but I took one of the corn dodgers and gave it to Little Blackie to see if he would eat it. He relished it and I gave him another. Rooster said horses particularly liked the salt that was in them. He directed me to wear my slicker.

Sunrise was only a pale yellow glow through the overcast but such as it was it found us mounted and moving once again. The snow came thicker and the flakes grew bigger, as big as goose feathers, and they were not falling down like rain but rather flying dead level into our faces. In the space of four hours it collected on the ground to a depth of six or seven inches.

Out in the open places the trail was hard to follow and we stopped often so that Rooster could get his bearings. This was a hard job because the ground told him nothing and he could not see distant landmarks. Indeed at times we could see only a few feet in any direction. His spyglass was useless. We came across no people and no houses. Our progress was very slow.

There was no great question of getting lost because Rooster had a compass and as long as we kept a southwesterly course we would sooner or later strike the Texas Road and the M. K. & T. Railroad tracks. But it was inconvenient not being able to keep the regular trail, and with the snow the horses ran the danger of stepping into holes.

Along about noon we stopped at a stream on the lee side of a mountain to water the horses. There we found some small relief from the wind and snow. I believe these were the San Bois Mountains. I passed the balance of my cheese around and Rooster shared his candy. With that we made our dinner. While we were stretching our legs at that place we heard some flapping noises down the stream and LaBoeuf went into the woods to investigate. He found a flock of turkeys roosting in a tree and shot one of them with his Sharps rifle. The bird was considerably ripped up. It was a hen weighing about seven pounds. LaBoeuf gutted it and cut its head off and tied it to his saddle.

Rooster allowed that we could not now reach McAlester's store before dark and that our best course was to bear west for a "dugout" that some squatter had built not far from the Texas Road. No one occupied the place, he said, and we could find shelter there for the night. Tomorrow we could make our way south on the Texas Road which was broad and packed clear and hard from cattle herds and freighter wagons. There would be little risk of crippling a horse on that highway.

After our rest we departed in single file with Rooster's big horse breaking the trail. Little Blackie had no need for my guidance and I looped the ends of the reins around the saddle horn and withdrew my cold hands into the sleeves of my many coats. We surprised a herd of deer feeding off the bark of saplings and LaBoeuf went for his rifle again but they had flown before he could get it unlimbered.

By and by the snow let up and yet our progress was still limited to a walk. It was good dark when we came to the "dugout." We had a little light from a moon that was in and out of the clouds.

The dugout stood at the narrow end of a V-shaped hollow or valley. I had never before seen such a dwelling. It was small, only about ten feet by twenty feet, and half of it was sunk back into a clay bank, like a cave. The part that was sticking out was made of poles and sod and the roof was also of sod, supported by a ridge pole in the center. A brush-arbor shed and cave adjoined it for livestock. There was a sufficiency of timber here for a log cabin, although mostly hardwood. I suppose too that the man who built the thing was in a hurry and wanted for proper tools. A "cockeyed" chimney of sticks and mud stuck up through the bank at the rear of the house. It put me in mind of something made by a water bird, some cliff martin or a swift, although the work of those little feathered masons (who know not the use of a spirit level) is a sight more artful.

We were surprised to see smoke and sparks coming from the chimney. Light showed through the cracks around the door, which was a low, crude thing hung to the sill by leather hinges. There was no window.

We had halted in a cedar brake. Rooster dismounted and told us to wait. He took his Winchester repeating rifle and approached the door. He made a lot of noise as his boots broke through the crust that had now formed on top of the snow.

When he was about twenty feet from the dugout

the door opened just a few inches. A man's face appeared in the light and a hand came out holding a revolver. Rooster stopped. The face said, "Who is it out there?" Rooster said, "We are looking for shelter. There is three of us." The face in the door said, "There is no room for you here." The door closed and in a moment the light inside went out.

Rooster turned to us and made a beckoning signal. LaBoeuf dismounted and went to join him. I made a move to go but LaBoeuf told me to stay in the cover of the brake and hold the horses.

Rooster took off his deerskin jacket and gave it to LaBoeuf and sent him up on the clay bank to cover the chimney. Then Rooster moved about ten feet to the side and got down on one knee with his rifle at the ready. The jacket made a good damper and soon smoke could be seen curling out around the door. There were raised voices inside and then a hissing noise as of water being thrown on fire and coals.

The door was flung open and there came two fiery blasts from a shotgun. It scared me nearly to death. I heard the shot falling through tree branches. Rooster returned the volley with several shots from his rifle. There was a yelp of pain from inside and the door was slammed to again.

"I am a Federal officer!" said Rooster. "Who all is in there? Speak up and be quick about it!"

"A Methodist and a son of a bitch!" was the insolent reply. "Keep riding!"

"Is that Emmett Quincy?" said Rooster.

"We don't know any Emmett Quincy!"

"Quincy, I know it is you! Listen to me! This is Rooster Cogburn! Columbus Potter and five more marshals is out here with me! We have got a bucket of coal oil! In one minute we will burn you out from both ends! Chuck your arms out clear and come out with your hands locked on your head and you will not be harmed! Oncet that coal oil goes down the chimney we are killing everything that comes out the door!"

"There is only three of you!"

"You go ahead and bet your life on it! How many is in there?"

"Moon can't walk! He is hit!"

"Drag him out! Light that lamp!"

"What kind of papers have you got on me?"

"I don't have no papers on you! You better move, boy! How many is in there?"

"Just me and Moon! Tell them other officers to be careful with their guns! We are coming out!"

A light showed again from inside. The door was pulled back and a shotgun and two revolvers were pitched out. The two men came out with one limping and holding to the other. Rooster and LaBoeuf made them lie down on their bellies in the snow while they were searched for more weapons. The one called Quincy had a bowie knife in one boot and a little two-shot gambler's pistol in the other. He said he had forgotten they were there but this did not keep Rooster from giving him a kick.

I came up with the horses and LaBoeuf took them into the stock shelter. Rooster poked the two men into the dugout with his rifle. They were young men in their twenties. The one called Moon was pale and frightened and looked no more dangerous than a fat puppy. He had been shot in the thigh and his trouser leg was bloody. The man Quincy had a long, thin face with eyes that were narrow and foreign-looking. He reminded me of some of those Slovak people that came in here a few years ago to cut barrel staves. The ones that stayed have made good citizens. People from those countries are usually Catholics if they are anything. They love candles and beads.

Rooster gave Moon a blue handkerchief to tie around his leg and then he bound the two men together with steel handcuffs and had them sit side by side on a bench. The only furniture in the place was a low table of adzed logs standing on pegs, and a bench on either side of it. I flapped a tow sack in the open door in an effort to clear the smoke out. A pot of coffee had been thrown into the fireplace but there were still some live coals and sticks around the edges and I stirred them up into a blaze again.

There was another pot in the fireplace too, a big one, a two-gallon pot, and it was filled with a mess that looked like hominy. Rooster tasted it with a spoon and said it was an Indian dish called sofky. He offered me some and said it was good. But it had trash in it and I declined.

"Was you boys looking for company?" he said.

"That is our supper and breakfast both," said Quincy. "I like a big breakfast."

"I would love to watch you eat breakfast."

"Sofky always cooks up bigger than you think."

"What are you boys up to outside of stealing stock and peddling spirits? You are way too jumpy."

"You said you didn't have no papers on us," replied Quincy.

"I don't have none on you by name," said Rooster. "I got some John Doe warrants on a few jobs I could tailor up for you. Resisting a Federal officer too. That's a year right there."

"We didn't know it was you. It might have been some crazy man out there."

Moon said, "My leg hurts."

Rooster said, "I bet it does. Set right still and it won't bleed so bad."

Quincy said, "We didn't know who it was out there. A night like this. We was drinking some and the weather spooked us. Anybody can say he is a marshal. Where is all the other officers?"

"I misled you there, Quincy. When was the last time you seen your old pard Ned Pepper?"

"Ned Pepper?" said the stock thief. "I don't know him. Who is he?"

"I think you know him," said Rooster. "I know you have heard of him. Everybody has heard of him."

"I never heard of him."

"He used to work for Mr. Burlingame. Didn't you work for him a while?"

"Yes, and I quit him like everybody else has done. He runs off all his good help, he is so close. The old skinflint. I wish he was in hell with his back broke. I don't remember any Ned Pepper."

Rooster said, "They say Ned was a mighty good drover. I am surprised you don't remember him. He is a little feisty fellow, nervous and quick. His lip is all messed up."

"That don't bring anybody to mind. A funny lip."

"He didn't always have it. I think you know him. Now here is something else. There is a new boy running with Ned. He is short himself and he has got a powder mark on his face, a black place. He calls himself Chaney or Chelmsford sometimes. He carries a Henry rifle."

"That don't bring anybody to mind," said Quincy. "A black mark. I would remember something like that."

"You don't know anything I want to know, do you?"

"No, and if I did I would not blow."

"Well, you think on it some, Quincy. You too, Moon."

Moon said, "I always try to help out the law if it

won't harm my friends. I don't know them boys. I would like to help you if I could."

"If you don't help me I will take you both back to Judge Parker," said Rooster. "By the time we get to Fort Smith that leg will be swelled up as tight as Dick's hatband. It will be mortified and they will cut it off. Then if you live I will get you two or three years in the Federal House up in Detroit."

"You are trying to get at me," said Moon.

"They will teach you how to read and write up there but the rest of it is not so good," said Rooster. "You don't have to go if you don't want to. If you give me some good information on Ned I will take you to McAlester's tomorrow and you can get that ball out of your leg. Then I will give you three days to clear the Territory. They have a lot of fat stock in Texas and you boys can do well there."

Moon said, "We can't go to Texas."

Quincy said, "Now don't go to flapping your mouth, Moon. It is best to let me do the talking."

"I can't set still. My leg is giving me fits."

Rooster got his bottle of whiskey and poured some in a cup for the young stock thief. "If you listen to Quincy, son, you will die or lose your leg," said he. "Quincy ain't hurting."

Quincy said, "Don't let him spook you, Moon. You must be a soldier. We will get clear of this."

LaBoeuf came in lugging our bedrolls and other traps. He said, "There are six horses out there in that cave, Cogburn."

"What kind of horses?" said Rooster.

"They look like right good mounts to me. I think they are all shod."

Rooster questioned the thieves about the horses and Quincy claimed they had bought them at Fort Gibson and were taking them down to sell to the Indian police called the Choctaw Light Horse. But he could show no bill of sale or otherwise prove the property and Rooster did not believe the story. Quincy grew sullen and would answer no further questions.

I was sent out to gather firewood and I took the lamp, or rather the bull's-eye lantern, for that was what it was, and kicked about in the snow and turned up some sticks and fallen saplings. I had no ax or hatchet and I dragged the pieces in whole, making several trips.

Rooster made another pot of coffee. He put me to slicing up the salt meat and corn dodgers, now frozen hard, and he directed Quincy to pick the feathers from the turkey and cut it up for frying. LaBoeuf wanted to roast the bird over the open fire but Rooster said it was not fat enough for that and would come out tough and dry.

I sat on a bench on one side of the table and the thieves sat on the other side, their manacled hands resting between them up on the table. The thieves had made pallets on the dirt floor by the fireplace and now Rooster and LaBoeuf sat on these blankets with their rifles in their laps, taking their ease. There were holes in the walls where the sod had fallen away and the wind came whistling through these places, making the lantern flicker a little, but the room was small and the fire gave off more than enough heat. Take it all around, we were rather cozily fixed.

I poured a can of scalding water over the stiff turkey but it was not enough to loosen all the feathers. Quincy picked them with his free hand and held the bird steady with the other. He grumbled over the awkwardness of the task. When the picking was done he cut the bird up into frying pieces with his big bowie knife and he showed his spite by doing a poor job of it. He made rough and careless chops instead of clean cuts.

Moon drank whiskey and whimpered from the pain in his leg. I felt sorry for him. Once he caught me stealing glances at him and he said, "What are you looking at?" It was a foolish question and I made no reply. He said, "Who are you? What are you doing here? What is this girl doing here?"

I said, "I am Mattie Ross of near Dardanelle, Arkansas. Now I will ask you a question. What made you become a stock thief?"

He said again, "What is this girl doing here?"

Rooster said, "She is with me."

"She is with both of us," said LaBoeuf.

Moon said, "It don't look right to me. I don't understand it."

I said, "The man Chaney, the man with the

marked face, killed my father. He was a whiskey drinker like you. It led to killing in the end. If you will answer the marshal's questions he will help you. I have a good lawyer at home and he will help you too."

"I am puzzled by this."

Quincy said, "Don't get to jawing with these people, Moon."

I said, "I don't like the way you look."

Quincy stopped his work. He said, "Are you talking to me, runt?"

I said, "Yes, and I will say it again. I don't like the way you look and I don't like the way you are cutting up that turkey. I hope you go to jail. My lawyer will not help you."

Quincy grinned and made a gesture with the knife as though to cut me. He said, "You are a fine one to talk about looks. You look like somebody has worked you over with the ugly stick."

I said, "Rooster, this Quincy is making a mess out of the turkey. He has got the bones all splintered up with the marrow showing."

Rooster said, "Do the job right, Quincy. I will have you eating feathers."

"I don't know nothing about this kind of work," said Quincy.

"A man that can skin a beef at night as fast as you can ought to be able to butcher a turkey," said Rooster.

Moon said, "I got to have me a doctor."

Quincy said, "Let up on that drinking. It is making you silly."

LaBoeuf said, "If we don't separate those two we are not going to get anything. The one has got a hold on the other."

Rooster said, "Moon is coming around. A young fellow like him don't want to lose his leg. He is too young to be getting about on a willow peg. He loves dancing and sport."

"You are trying to get at me," said Moon.

"I am getting at you with the truth," said Rooster.

In a few minutes Moon leaned over to whisper a confidence into Quincy's ear. "None of that," said Rooster, raising his rifle. "If you have anything on your mind we will all hear it."

Moon said, "We seen Ned and Haze just two days ago."

"Don't act the fool!" said Quincy. "If you blow I will kill you."

But Moon went on. "I am played out," said he. "I must have a doctor. I will tell what I know."

With that, Quincy brought the bowie knife down on Moon's cuffed hand and chopped off four fingers which flew up before my eyes like chips from a log. Moon screamed and a rifle ball shattered the lantern in front of me and struck Quincy in the neck, causing hot blood to spurt on my face. My thought was: *I am better out of this.* I tumbled backward from the bench and sought a place of safety on the dirt floor.

Rooster and LaBoeuf sprang to where I lay and when they ascertained that I was not hurt they went to the fallen thieves. Quincy was insensible and dead or dying and Moon was bleeding terribly from his hand and from a mortal puncture in the breast that Quincy gave him before they fell.

"Oh Lord, I am dying!" said he.

Rooster struck a match for light and told me to fetch a pine knot from the fireplace. I found a good long piece and lit it and brought it back, a smoky torch to illuminate a dreadful scene. Rooster removed the handcuff from the poor young man's wrist.

"Do something! Help me!" were his cries.

"I can do nothing for you, son," said Rooster. "Your pard has killed you and I have done for him."

"Don't leave me laying here. Don't let the wolves make an end of me."

"I will see you are buried right, though the ground is hard," said Rooster. "You must tell me about Ned. Where did you see him?"

"We seen him two days ago at McAlester's, him and Haze. They are coming here tonight to get remounts and supper. They are robbing the Katy Flyer at Wagoner's Switch if the snow don't stop them."

"There is four of them?"

"They wanted four horses, that is all I know. Ned was Quincy's friend, not mine. I would not blow on a friend. I was afraid there would be shooting and I would not have a chance bound up like I was. I am bold in a fight."

Rooster said, "Did you see a man with a black mark on his face?"

"I didn't see nobody but Ned and Haze. When it comes to a fight I am right there where it is warmest but if I have time to think on it I am not true. Quincy hated all the laws but he was true to his friends."

"What time did they say they would be here?"

"I looked for them before now. My brother is George Garrett. He is a Methodist circuit rider in south Texas. I want you to sell my traps, Rooster, and send the money to him in care of the district superintendent in Austin. The dun horse is mine, I paid for him. We got them others last night at Mr. Burlingame's."

I said, "Do you want us to tell your brother what happened to you?"

He said, "It don't matter about that. He knows I am on the scout. I will meet him later walking the streets of Glory."

Rooster said, "Don't be looking for Quincy."

"Quincy was always square with me," said Moon. "He never played me false until he killed me. Let me have a drink of cold water."

LaBoeuf brought him some water in a cup. Moon reached for it with the bloody stump and then took it with the other hand. He said, "It feels like I still have fingers there but I don't." He drank deep and it caused him pain. He talked a little more but in a rambling manner and to no sensible purpose. He did not respond to questions. Here is what was in his eyes: *confusion*. Soon it was all up with him and he joined his friend in death. He looked about thirty pounds lighter.

LaBoeuf said, "I told you we should have separated them."

Rooster said nothing to that, not wishing to own he had made a mistake. He went through the pockets of the dead thieves and put such oddments as he found upon the table. The lantern was beyond repair and LaBoeuf brought out a candle from his saddle wallet and lit it and fixed it on the table. Rooster turned up a few coins and cartridges and notes of paper money and a picture of a pretty girl torn from an illustrated paper and pocket knives and a plug of tobacco. He also found a California gold piece in Quincy's vest pocket.

I fairly shouted when I saw it. "That is my father's gold piece!" said I. "Let me have it!"

It was not a round coin but a rectangular slug of gold that was minted in "The Golden State" and was worth thirty-six dollars and some few cents. Rooster said, "I never seen a piece like this before. Are you sure it is the one?" I said, "Yes, Grandfather Spurling gave Papa two of these when he married Mama. That scoundrel Chaney has still got the other one. We are on his trail for certain!"

"We are on Ned's trail anyhow," said Rooster. "I expect it is the same thing. I wonder how Quincy got aholt of this. Is this Chaney a gambler?"

LaBoeuf said, "He likes a game of cards. I reckon Ned has called off the robbery if he is not here by now."

"Well, we won't count on that," said Rooster. "Saddle the horses and I will lug these boys out."

"Do you aim to run?" said LaBoeuf.

Rooster turned a glittering eye on him. "I aim to do what I come out here to do," said he. "Saddle the horses."

Rooster directed me to straighten up the inside of the dugout. He carried the bodies out and concealed them in the woods. I sacked up the turkey fragments and pitched the wrecked lantern into the fireplace and stirred around on the dirt floor with a stick to cover the blood. Rooster was planning an ambush.

When he came back from his second trip to the woods he brought a load of limbs for the fireplace. He built up a big fire so there would be light and smoke and indicate that the cabin was occupied. Then we went out and joined LaBoeuf and the horses in the brush arbor. This dwelling, as I have said, was set back in a hollow where two slopes pinched together in a kind of V. It was a good place for what Rooster had in mind.

He directed LaBoeuf to take his horse and find a position up on the north slope about midway along one stroke of the V, and explained that he would take up a corresponding position on the south slope. Nothing was said about me with regard to the plan and I elected to stay with Rooster.

He said to LaBoeuf, "Find you a good place up yonder and then don't move about. Don't shoot unless you hear me shoot. What we want is to get them all in the dugout. I will kill the last one to go in and then we will have them in a barrel."

"You will shoot him in the back?" asked LaBoeuf.

"It will give them to know our intentions is serious. These ain't chicken thieves. I don't want you to start shooting unless they break. After my first shot I will call down and see if they will be taken alive. If they won't we will shoot them as they come out."

"There is nothing in this plan but a lot of killing," said LaBoeuf. "We want Chelmsford alive, don't we? You are not giving them any show."

"It is no use giving Ned and Haze a show. If they are taken they will hang and they know it. They will go for a fight every time. The others may be chickenhearted and give up, I don't know. Another thing, we don't know how many there is. I do know there is just two of us."

"Why don't I try to wing Chelmsford before he gets inside?"

"I don't like that," said Rooster. "If there is any shooting before they get in that dugout we are likely to come up with a empty sack. I want Ned too. I want all of them."

"All right," said LaBoeuf. "But if they do break I am going for Chelmsford."

"You are liable to kill him with that big Sharps no matter where you hit him. You go for Ned and I will try to nick this Chaney in the legs."

"What does Ned look like?"

"He is a little fellow. I don't know what he will be riding. He will be doing a lot of talking. Just go for the littlest one."

"What if they hole up in there for a siege? They may figure on staying till dark and then breaking."

"I don't think they will," said Rooster. "Now don't keep on with this. Get on up there. If something queer turns up you will just have to use your head."

"How long will we wait?"

"Till daylight anyhow."

"I don't think they are coming now."

"Well, you may be right. Now move. Keep your eyes open and your horse quiet. Don't go to sleep and don't get the 'jimjams.'"

Rooster took a cedar bough and brushed around over all our tracks in front of the dugout. Then we took our horses and led them up the hill in a roundabout route along a rocky stream bed. We went over the crest and Rooster posted me there with the horses. He told me to talk to them or give them some oats or put my hand over their nostrils if they started blowing or neighing. He put some corn dodgers in his pocket and left to go for his ambush position.

I said, "I cannot see anything from here."

He said, "This is where I want you to stay."

"I am going with you where I can see something."

"You will do like I tell you."

"The horses will be all right."

"You have not seen enough killing tonight?"

"I am not staying here by myself."

We started back over the ridge together. I said, "Wait, I will go back and get my revolver," but he grabbed me roughly and pulled me along after him and I left the pistol behind. He found us a place behind a big log that offered a good view of the hollow and the dugout. We kicked the snow back so that we could rest on the leaves underneath. Rooster loaded his rifle from a sack of cartridges and placed the sack on the log where he would have it ready at hand. He got out his revolver and put a cartridge into the one chamber that he kept empty under the hammer. The same shells fit his pistol and rifle alike. I thought you had to have different kinds. I bunched myself up inside the slicker and rested my head against the log. Rooster ate a corn dodger and offered me one.

I said, "Strike a match and let me look at it first."

"What for?" said he.

"There was blood on some of them."

"We ain't striking no matches."

"I don't want it then. Let me have some taffy."

"It is all gone."

I tried to sleep but it was too cold. I cannot sleep when my feet are cold. I asked Rooster what he had done before he became a Federal marshal.

"I done everything but keep school," said he.

"What was one thing that you did?" said I.

"I skinned buffalo and killed wolves for bounty out on the Yellow House Creek in Texas. I seen wolves out there that weighed a hundred and fifty pounds."

"Did you like it?"

"It paid well enough but I didn't like that open country. Too much wind to suit me. There ain't but about six trees between there and Canada. Some people like it fine. Everything that grows out there has got stickers on it."

"Have you ever been to California?"

"I never got out there."

"My Grandfather Spurling lives in Monterey, California. He owns a store there and he can look out his window any time he wants to and see the blue ocean. He sends me five dollars every Christmas. He has buried two wives and is now married to one called Jenny who is thirty-one years of age. That is one year younger than Mama. Mama will not even say her name."

"I fooled around in Colorado for a spell but I never got out to California. I freighted supplies for a man named Cook out of Denver."

"Did you fight in the war?"

"Yes, I did."

"Papa did too. He was a good soldier."

"I expect he was."

"Did you know him?"

"No, where was he?"

"He fought at Elkhorn Tavern in Arkansas and was badly wounded at Chickamauga up in the state of Tennessee. He came home after that and nearly died on the way. He served in General Churchill's brigade."

"I was mostly in Missouri."

"Did you lose your eye in the war?"

"I lost it in the fight at Lone Jack out of Kansas City. My horse was down too and I was all but blind. Cole Younger crawled out under a hail of fire and pulled me back. Poor Cole, he and Bob and Jim are now doing life in the Minnesota pen. You watch, when the truth is known, they will find it was Jesse W. James that shot that cashier in Northfield."

"Do you know Jesse James?"

"I don't remember him. Potter tells me he was with us at Centralia and killed a Yankee major there. Potter said he was a mean little viper then, though he was only a boy. Said he was meaner than Frank. That is going some, if it be so. I remember Frank well. We called him Buck then. I don't remember Jesse."

"Now you are working for the Yankees."

"Well, the times has changed since Betsy died. I would have never thought it back then. The Red Legs from Kansas burned my folks out and took their stock. They didn't have nothing to eat but clabber and roasting ears. You can eat a peck of roasting ears and go to bed hungry."

"What did you do when the war was over?"

"Well, I will tell you what I done. When we heard they had all give up in Virginia, Potter and me rode into Independence and turned over our arms. They asked us was we ready to respect the Government in Washington city and take a oath to the Stars and Stripes. We said yes, we was about ready. We done it, we swallowed the puppy, but they wouldn't let us go right then. They give us a one-day parole and told us to report back in the morning. We heard there was a Kansas major coming in that night to look over everybody for bushwhackers."

"What are bushwhackers?"

"I don't know. That is what they called us. Anyhow, we was not easy about that Kansas major. We didn't know but what he would lock us up or worse, us having rode with Bill Anderson and Captain Quantrill. Potter lifted a revolver from a office and we lit out that night on two government mules. I am still traveling on the one-day parole and I reckon that jayhawker is waiting yet. Now our clothes was rags and we didn't have the price of a plug of tobacco between us. About eight mile out of town we run into a Federal captain and three soldiers. They wanted to know if they was on the right road for Kansas City. That captain was a paymaster, and we relieved them gents of over four thousand in coin. They squealed like it was their own. It didn't belong to nobody but the Government and we needed a road stake."

"Four thousand dollars?"

"Yes, and all in gold. We got their horses too. Potter taken his half of the money and went down to Arkansas. I went to Cairo, Illinois, with mine and started calling myself Burroughs and bought a eating place called *The Green Frog* and married a grass widow. It had one billiard table. We served ladies and men both, but mostly men."

"I didn't know you had a wife."

"Well, I don't now. She taken a notion she wanted me to be a lawyer. Running a eating place was too low-down for her. She bought a heavy book called *Daniels on Negotiable Instruments* and set me to reading it. I never could get a grip on it. Old Daniels pinned me every time. My drinking picked up and I commenced staying away two and three days at a time with my friends. My wife did not crave the society of my river friends. She got a bellyful of it and decided she would go back to her first husband who was clerking in a hardware store over in Paducah. She said, 'Goodbye, Reuben, a love for decency does not abide in you.' There is

151

your divorced woman talking about decency. I told her, I said, 'Goodbye, Nola, I hope that little nail-selling bastard will make you happy this time.' She took my boy with her too. He never did like me anyhow. I guess I did speak awful rough to him but I didn't mean nothing by it. You would not want to see a clumsier child than Horace. I bet he broke forty cups."

"What happened to *The Green Frog?*"

"I tried to run it myself for a while but I couldn't keep good help and I never did learn how to buy meat. I didn't know what I was doing. I was like a man fighting bees. Finally I just give up and sold it for nine hundred dollars and went out to see the country. That was when I went out to the staked plains of Texas and shot buffalo with Vernon Shaftoe and a Flathead Indian called Olly. The Mormons had run Shaftoe out of Great Salt Lake City but don't ask me about what it was for. Call it a misunderstanding and let it go at that. There is no use in you asking me questions about it, for I will not answer them. Olly and me both taken a solemn oath to keep silent. Well, sir, the big shaggies is about all gone. It is a damned shame. I would give three dollars right now for a pickled buffalo tongue."

"They never did get you for stealing that money?"

"I didn't look on it as stealing."

"That was what it was. It didn't belong to you."

152

"It never troubled me in that way. I sleep like a baby. Have for years."

"Colonel Stonehill said you were a road agent before you got to be a marshal."

"I wondered who was spreading that talk. That old gentleman would do better minding his own business."

"Then it is just talk."

"It is very little more than that. I found myself one pretty spring day in Las Vegas, New Mexico, in need of a road stake and I robbed one of them little high-interest banks there. Thought I was doing a good service. You can't rob a thief, can you? I never robbed no citizens. I never taken a man's watch."

"It is all stealing," said I.

"That was the position they taken in New Mexico," said he. "I had to fly for my life. Three fights in one day. Bo was a strong colt then and there was not a horse in that territory could run him in the ground. But I did not appreciate being chased and shot at like a thief. When the posse had thinned down to about seven men I turned Bo around and taken the reins in my teeth and rode right at them boys firing them two navy sixes I carry on my saddle. I guess they was all married men who loved their families as they scattered and run for home."

"That is hard to believe."

"What is?"

"One man riding at seven men like that."

"It is true enough. We done it in the war. I seen a dozen bold riders stampede a full troop of regular cavalry. You go for a man hard enough and fast enough and he don't have time to think about how many is with him, he thinks about himself and how he may get clear out of the wrath that is about to set down on him."

"I think you are 'stretching the blanket.'"

"Well, that was the way of it. Me and Bo walked into Texas, we didn't run. I might not do it today. I am older and stouter and so is Bo. I lost my money to some quarter-mile horse racers out there in Texas and followed them highbinders across Red River up in the Chickasaw Nation and lost their trail. That was when I tied up with a man named Fogelson who was taking a herd of beef to Kansas. We had a pretty time with them steers. It rained every night and the grass was spongy and rank. It was cloudy by day and the mosquitoes eat us up. Fogelson abused us like a stepfather. We didn't know what sleep was. When we got to the South Canadian it was all out of the banks but Fogelson had a time contract and he wouldn't wait. He said, 'Boys, we are going across.' We lost near about seventy head getting across and counted ourselves lucky. Lost our wagon too; we done without bread and coffee after that. It was the same story all over again at the North Canadian. 'Boys, we are going across.' Some of them steers got bogged in the mud on the other side and I was pulling them free. Bo was about played out and I hollered up for that Hutchens to come help me. He was sitting up there on his horse smoking a pipe. Now, he wasn't a regular drover. He was from Philadelphia, Pennsylvania, and he had some interest in the herd. He said, 'Do it yourself. That's what you are paid for.' I pulled down on him right there. It was not the thing to do but I was wore out and hadn't had no coffee. It didn't hurt him bad, the ball just skinned his head and he bit his pipe in two, yet nothing would do but he would have the law. There wasn't no law out there and Fogelson told him as much, so Hutchens had me disarmed and him and two drovers taken me over to Fort Reno. Now the army didn't care nothing about his private quarrels but there happened to be two Federal marshals there picking up some whiskey peddlers. One of them marshals was Potter."

I was just about asleep. Rooster nudged me and said, "I say one of them marshals was Potter."

"What?"

"One of them two marshals at Fort Reno was Potter."

"It was your friend from the war? The same one?"

"Yes, it was Columbus Potter in the flesh. I was glad to see him. He didn't let on he knowed me. He told Hutchens he would take me in charge and see I was prosecuted. Hutchens said he would come

155

back by Fort Smith when his business was done in Kansas and appear against me. Potter told him his statement right there was good enough to convict me of assault. Hutchens said he never heard of a court where they didn't need witnesses. Potter said they had found it saved time. We come on over to Fort Smith and Potter got me commissioned as deputy marshal. Jo Shelby had vouched for him to the chief marshal and got him the job. General Shelby is in the railroad business up in Missouri now and he knows all these Republicans. He wrote a handsome letter for me too. Well, there is no beat of a good friend. Potter was a trump."

"Do you like being a marshal?"

"I believe I like it better than anything I done since the war. Anything beats droving. Nothing I like to do pays well."

"I don't think Chaney is going to show up."

"We will get him."

"I hope we get him tonight."

"You told me you loved coon hunting."

"I didn't expect it would be easy. I still hope we get him tonight and have it done with."

Rooster talked all night. I would doze off and wake up and he would still be talking. Some of his stories had too many people in them and were hard to follow but they helped to pass the hours and took my mind off the cold. I did not give credence to everything he said. He said he knew a woman in Sedalia, Missouri, who had stepped on a needle as a girl and nine years later the needle worked out of the thigh of her third child. He said it puzzled the doctors.

I was asleep when the bandits arrived. Rooster shook me awake and said, "Here they come." I gave a start and turned over on my stomach so I could peer over the log. It was false dawn and you could see broad shapes and outlines but you could not make out details. The riders were strung out and they were laughing and talking amongst themselves. I counted them. *Six!* Six armed men against two! They exercised no caution at all and my thought was: *Rooster's plan is working fine.* But when they were about fifty yards from the dugout they stopped. The fire inside the dugout had gone down but there was still a little string of smoke coming from the mud chimney.

Rooster whispered to me, "Do you see your man?"

I said, "I cannot see their faces."

He said, "That little one without the hat is Ned Pepper. He has lost his hat. He is riding foremost."

"What are they doing?"

"Looking about. Keep your head down."

Lucky Ned Pepper appeared to be wearing white trousers but I learned later that these were sheepskin "chaps." One of the bandits made a sound like a turkey gobbling. He waited and gobbled again and then another time, but of course there was no reply from the vacant dugout. Two of the bandits then rode up to the dugout and dismounted. One of them called out several times for Quincy. Rooster said, "That is Haze." The two men then entered the cabin with their arms ready. In a minute or so they came out and searched around outside. The man Haze called out repeatedly for Quincy and once he whooped like a man calling hogs. Then he called back to the bandits who had remained mounted, saying, "The horses are here. It looks like Moon and Quincy have stepped out."

"Stepped out where?" inquired the bandit chieftain, Lucky Ned Pepper.

"I can make nothing from the sign," said the man Haze. "There is six horses in there. There is a pot of sofky in the fireplace but the fire is down. It beats me. Maybe they are out tracking game in the snow."

Lucky Ned Pepper said, "Quincy would not leave a warm fire to go track a rabbit at night. That is no answer at all."

Haze said, "The snow is all stirred up out here in front. Come and see what you make of it, Ned."

The man that was with Haze said, "What difference does it make? Let us change horses and get on out of here. We can get something to eat at Ma's place."

Lucky Ned Pepper said, "Let me think a minute."

The man that was with Haze said, "We are wasting time that is better spent riding. We have lost enough time in this snow and left a broad track as well."

When the man spoke the second time Rooster identified him as a Mexican gambler from Fort Worth, Texas, who called himself The Original Greaser Bob. He did not talk the Mexican language, though I suppose he knew it. I looked hard at the mounted bandits but mere effort was not enough to pierce the shadows and make out faces. Nor could I tell much from their physical attitudes as they were wearing heavy coats and big hats and their horses were ever milling about. I did not recognize Papa's horse, Judy.

Lucky Ned Pepper pulled one of his revolvers and fired it rapidly three times in the air. The noise rumbled in the hollow and there followed an expectant silence.

In a moment there came a loud report from the opposite ridge and Lucky Ned Pepper's horse was felled as though from a poleax. Then more shots from the ridge and the bandits were seized with panic and confusion. It was LaBoeuf over there firing his heavy rifle as fast as he could load it.

Rooster cursed and rose to his feet and commenced firing and pumping his Winchester repeating rifle. He shot Haze and The Original Greaser before they could mount their horses. Haze was killed where he stood. The hot cartridge cases from Rooster's rifle fell on my hand and I jerked it away. When he turned to direct his fire on the other bandits, The Original Greaser, who was only wounded, got to his feet and caught his horse and rode out behind the others. He was clinging to the far side of his horse with one leg thrown over for support. If you had not followed the entire "stunt" from start to finish as I had done, you would have thought the horse was riderless. That is how he escaped Rooster's attention. I was "mesmerized" and proved to be of no help.

Now I will back up and tell of the others. Lucky Ned Pepper was bowled over with his horse but he quickly crawled from under the dead beast and cut his saddle wallets free with a knife. The other three bandits had already spurred their horses away from the deadly cockpit, as I may call it, and they were firing their rifles and revolvers at LaBoeuf on the run. Rooster and I were behind them and a good deal farther away from them than LaBoeuf. As far as I know, not a shot was fired at us.

Lucky Ned Pepper shouted after the riders and pursued them on foot in a zigzag manner. He carried the saddle wallets over one arm and a revolver in the other hand. Rooster could not hit him. The bandit was well named "Lucky," and his luck was not through running yet. In all the booming and smoke and confusion, one of his men chanced to hear his cries and he wheeled his horse about and made a dash back to pick up his boss. Just as the man reached Lucky Ned Pepper and leaned over to extend a hand to help him aboard he was knocked clean from the saddle by a well-placed shot from LaBoeuf's powerful rifle. Lucky Ned Pepper expertly swung aboard in the man's place without so much as a word or a parting glance at the fallen friend who had dared to come back and save him. He rode low and the trick-riding Mexican gambler followed him out and they were gone. The scrap did not last as long as it has taken me to describe it.

Rooster told me to get the horses. He ran down the hill on foot.

The bandits had left two of their number behind and we had forced the others to continue their flight on jaded ponies, but I thought we had little reason to congratulate ourselves. The bandits in the snow were dead men and could "tell no tales." We had not identified Chaney among those who escaped. Was he with them? Were we really on his trail? Also, we found that Lucky Ned Pepper had made off with the greater part of the loot from the train robbery.

The thing might have fallen out more to our advantage had LaBoeuf not started the fight prematurely. But I cannot be sure. I think Lucky Ned Pepper had no intention of entering that dugout, or indeed of approaching it any closer, when he discovered the two stock thieves unaccountably missing. So our plan had miscarried in any case. Rooster was disposed to place all the blame on LaBoeuf.

When I reached the bottom of the hill with the horses he was cursing the Texan to his face. I am certain the two must have come to blows if LaBoeuf had not been distracted from a painful wound. A ball had struck his rifle stock and splinters of wood and lead had torn the soft flesh of his upper arm. He said he had not been able to see well from his position and was moving to a better place when he heard the three signal shots fired by Lucky Ned Pepper. He thought the fight was joined and he stood up from a crouch and threw a quick shot down at the man he had rightly sized up as the bandit chieftain.

Rooster called it a likely story and charged that LaBoeuf had fallen asleep and had started shooting from panic when the signal shots awakened him. I thought it was in LaBoeuf's favor that his first shot had struck and killed Lucky Ned Pepper's horse. If he had been shooting from panic would he have come so near to hitting the bandit chieftain with his first shot? On the other hand, he claimed to be an experienced officer and rifleman, and if he had been alert and had taken a deliberate shot would he not have hit his mark? Only LaBoeuf knew the truth of the matter. I grew impatient with their wrangling over the point. I think Rooster was angry because the play had been taken away from him and because Lucky Ned Pepper had beaten him once again.

The two officers made no move to give pursuit to

the robber band and I suggested that we had better make such a move. Rooster said he knew where they were going to earth and he did not wish to risk riding into an ambush along the way. LaBoeuf made the point that our horses were fresh and theirs jaded. He said we could track them easily and overtake them in short order. But Rooster wanted to take the stolen horses and the dead bandits down to McAlester's and establish a prior claim to any reward the M. K. & T. Railroad might offer. Scores of marshals and railroad detectives and informers would soon be in on the game, said he.

LaBoeuf was rubbing snow on the torn places of his arm to check the bleeding. He took off his neck cloth for use as a bandage but he could not manage it with one hand and I helped him.

Rooster watched me minister to the Texan's arm and he said, "That is nothing to do with you. Go inside and make some coffee."

I said, "This will not take long."

He said, "Let it go and make the coffee."

I said, "Why are you being so silly?"

He walked away and I finished binding up the arm. I heated up the sofky and picked the trash from it and boiled some coffee in the fireplace. LaBoeuf joined Rooster in the stock cave and they strung the six horses together with halters and a long manila rope and lashed the four dead bodies across their backs like sacks of corn. The dun horse belonging to Moon bolted and bared his teeth and would not permit his dead master to be placed on his back. A less sensitive horse was found to serve.

Rooster could not identify the man who had returned to rescue Lucky Ned Pepper. I say "man." He was really only a boy, not much older than I. His mouth was open and I could not bear to look at him. The man Haze was old with a sallow wrinkled face. They had a hard time breaking the revolver free from his "death grip."

The two officers found Haze's horse in the woods nearby. He was not injured. Right behind the saddle the horse was carrying two tow sacks, and in these sacks were about thirty-five watches, some ladies' rings, some pistols and around six hundred dollars in notes and coin. Loot from the passengers of the Katy Flyer! While searching over the ground where the bandits had made their fight, LaBoeuf turned up some copper cartridge cases. He showed them to Rooster.

I said, "What are they?"

Rooster said, "This one is a forty-four rim-fire from a Henry rifle."

Thus we had another clue. But we did not have Chaney. We had not even set eyes on him to know it. We took a hasty breakfast of the Indian hominy dish and departed the place.

It was only an hour's ride to the Texas Road. We made quite a caravan. If you had chanced to be riding up the Texas Road on that bright December morning you would have met two red-eyed peace officers and a sleepy youth from near Dardanelle, Arkansas, riding south at a walk and leading seven horses. Had you looked closely you would have seen that four of those horses were draped over with the corpses of armed robbers and stock thieves. We did in fact meet several travelers and they marveled and wondered at our grisly cargo.

Some of them had already heard news of the train robbery. One man, an Indian, told us that the robbers had realized seventeen thousand dollars in cash from the express car. Two men in a buggy told us their information put the figure at seventy thousand dollars. A great difference!

The accounts did agree roughly on the circumstances of the robbery. Here is what happened. The bandits broke the switch lock at Wagoner's Switch and forced the train onto a cattle siding. There they took the engineer and the fireman as hostages and threatened to kill them if the express clerk did not open the doors of his car. The clerk had spunk and refused to open the doors. The robbers killed the fireman. But the clerk still held fast. The robbers then blasted the door open with dynamite and the clerk was killed in the explosion. More dynamite was used to open the safe. While this was going on two bandits were walking through the coaches with cocked revolvers gathering up "booty" from the passengers. One man in a sleeping car protested the outrage and was assaulted and cut on the head with a pistol barrel. He was the only one they bothered except for the fireman and the express clerk. The bandits wore their hats low and had handkerchiefs tied over their faces but Lucky Ned Pepper was recognized by way of his small size and commanding manner. None of the others was identified. And that is how they robbed the Katy Flyer at Wagoner's Switch.

The riding was easy on the Texas Road. It was broad and had a good packed surface as Rooster had described it. The sun was out and the snow melted fast under the warm and welcome rays of "Old Sol."

As we rode along LaBoeuf commenced whistling tunes, perhaps to take his mind off his sore arm. Rooster said, "God damn a man that whistles!" It was the wrong thing to say if he wished it to stop. LaBoeuf then had to keep it up to show that he cared little for Rooster's opinion. After a while he took a Jew's harp from his pocket. He began to thump and twang upon it. He played fiddle tunes. He would announce, "Soldier's Joy," and play that. Then, "Johnny in the Low Ground," and play that. Then, "The Eighth of January," and play that. They all sounded pretty much like the same song. LaBoeuf said, "Is there anything you would particularly like to hear, Cogburn?" He was trying to get his "goat." Rooster gave no answer. LaBoeuf then played a few minstrel tunes and put the peculiar instrument away.

In a few minutes he asked Rooster this question, indicating the big revolvers in the saddle scabbards: "Did you carry those in the war?"

Rooster said, "I have had them a good long time."

LaBoeuf said, "I suppose you were with the cavalry."

Rooster said, "I forget just what they called it."

"I wanted to be cavalryman," said LaBoeuf, "but I was too young and didn't own a horse. I have always regretted it. I went in the army on my fifteenth birthday and saw the last six months of the war. My mother cried because my brothers had not been home in three years. They were off at the first tap of a drum. The army put me in the supply department and I counted beeves and sacked oats for General Kirby-Smith at Shreveport. It was no work for a soldier. I wanted to get out of the Trans-Mississippi Department and go east. I wanted to see some real fighting. Right toward the last I got an opportunity to travel up there with a commissary officer, Major Burks, who was being transferred to the Department of Virginia. There were twenty-five in our party and we got there in time for Five Forks and Petersburg and then it was all over. I have always regretted that I did not get to ride with Stuart or Forrest or some of the others. Shelby and Early."

Rooster said nothing.

I said, "It looks like six months would be enough for you."

LaBoeuf said, "No, it sounds boastful and foolish but it was not. I was almost sick when I heard of the surrender."

I said, "My father said he sure was glad to get home. He nearly died on the way."

LaBoeuf then said to Rooster, "It is hard to believe a man cannot remember where he served in the war. Do you not even remember your regiment?"

Rooster said, "I think they called it the bullet department. I was in it four years."

"You do not think much of me, do you, Cogburn?"

"I don't think about you at all when your mouth is closed."

"You are making a mistake about me."

"I don't like this kind of talk. It is like women talking."

"I was told in Fort Smith that you rode with Quantrill and that border gang."

Rooster made no reply.

LaBoeuf said, "I have heard they were not soldiers at all but murdering thieves."

Rooster said, "I have heard the same thing."

"I heard they murdered women and children at Lawrence, Kansas."

"I have heard that too. It is a damned lie."

"Were you there?"

"Where?"

"The Lawrence raid."

"There has been a lot of lies told about that."

"Do you deny they shot down soldiers and civilians alike and burned the town?"

"We missed Jim Lane. What army was you in, mister?"

"I was at Shreveport first with Kirby-Smith—"

"Yes, I heard about all them departments. What *side* was you on?"

"I was in the Army of Northern Virginia, Cogburn, and I don't have to hang my head when I say it. Now make another joke about it. You are only trying to put on a show for this girl Mattie with what you must think is a keen tongue."

"This is like women talking."

"Yes, that is the way. Make me out foolish in this girl's eyes."

"I think she has got you pretty well figured."

"You are making a mistake about me, Cogburn, and I do not appreciate the way you make conversation."

"That is nothing for you to worry about. That nor Captain Quantrill either."

"*Captain* Quantrill!"

"You had best let this go, LaBoeuf."

"Captain of what?"

"If you are looking for a fight I will accommodate you. If you are not you will let this alone."

"*Captain* Quantrill indeed!"

I rode up between them and said, "I have been thinking about something. Listen to this. There were six bandits and two stock thieves and yet only six horses at the dugout. What is the answer to that?"

Rooster said, "Six horses was all they needed."

I said, "Yes, but that six includes the horses belonging to Moon and Quincy. There were only four stolen horses."

Rooster said, "They would have taken them other two as well and exchanged them later. They have done it before."

"Then what would Moon and Quincy do for mounts?"

"They would have the six tired horses."

"Oh. I had forgotten about them."

"It was only a swap for a few days."

"I was thinking that Lucky Ned Pepper might have been planning to murder the two stock thieves. It would have been a treacherous scheme but then they could not inform against him. What do you think?"

"No, Ned would not do that."

"Why not? He and his desperate band killed a fireman and an express clerk on the Katy Flyer last night."

"Ned does not go around killing people if he has no good reason. If he has a good reason he kills them."

"You can think what you want to," said I. "I think betrayal was part of his scheme."

We reached J. J. McAlester's store about ten o'clock that morning. The people of the settlement turned out to see the dead bodies and there were gasps and murmurs over the spectacle of horror, made the worse by way of the winter morning being so sunny and cheerful. It must have been a trading day for there were several wagons and horses tied up about the store. The railroad tracks ran behind it. There was little more to the place than the store building and a few smaller frame and log structures of poor description, and yet if I am not mistaken this was at that time one of the best towns in the Choctaw Nation. The store is now part of the modern little city of McAlester, Oklahoma, where for a long time "coal was king." McAlester is also the international headquarters of the Order of the Rainbow for Girls.

There was no real doctor there at that time but there was a young Indian who had some medical training and was competent to set broken bones and dress gunshot wounds. LaBoeuf sought him out for treatment.

I went with Rooster, who searched out an Indian policeman of his acquaintance, a Captain Boots Finch of the Choctaw Light Horse. These police handled Indian crimes only, and where white men were involved the Light Horse had no authority. We found the captain in a small log house. He was sitting on a box by a stove getting his hair cut. He was a slender man about of an age with Rooster. He and the Indian barber were ignorant of the stir our arrival had caused.

Rooster came up behind the captain and goosed him in the ribs with both hands and said, "How is the people's health, Boots?"

The captain gave a start and reached for his pistol, and then he saw who it was. He said, "Well, I declare, Rooster. What brings you to town so early?"

"Is this town? I was thinking I was out of town."

Captain Finch laughed at the gibe. He said, "You must have traveled fast if you are here on that Wagoner's Switch business."

"That is the business right enough."

"It was little Ned Pepper and five others. I suppose you know that."

"Yes. How much did they get?"

"Mr. Smallwood says they got seventeen thousand dollars cash and a packet of registered mail from the safe. He has not got a total on the passenger claims. I am afraid you are on a cold trail here."

"When did you last see Ned?"

"I am told he passed through here two days ago. He and Haze and a Mexican on a round-bellied calico pony. I didn't see them myself. They won't be coming back this way."

Rooster said, "That Mexican was Greaser Bob."

"Is that the young one?"

"No, it's the old one, the Original Bob from Fort Worth."

"I heard he was badly shot in Denison and had given up his reckless ways."

"Bob is hard to kill. He won't stay shot. I am looking for another man. I think he is with Ned. He is short and has a black mark on his face and he carries a Henry rifle."

Captain Finch thought about it. He said, "No, the way I got it, there was only the three here. Haze and the Mexican and Ned. We are watching his woman's house. It is a waste of time and none of my business but I have sent a man out there."

Rooster said, "It is a waste of time all right. I know about where Ned is."

"Yes, I know too but it will take a hundred marshals to smoke him out of there."

"It won't take that many."

"It wouldn't take that many Choctaws. How many were in that marshals' party in August? Forty?"

"It was closer to fifty," said Rooster. "Joe Schmidt was running that game, or misrunning it. I am running this one."

"I am surprised the chief marshal would turn you loose on a hunt like this without supervision."

"He can't help himself this time."

Captain Finch said, "I could take you in there, Rooster, and show you how to bring Ned out."

"Could you now? Well, a Indian makes too much

noise to suit me. Don't you find it so, Gaspargoo?"

That was the barber's name. He laughed and put his hand over his mouth. Gaspargoo is also the name of a fish that makes fair eating.

I said to the captain, "Perhaps you are wondering who I am."

"Yes, I *was* wondering that," said he. "I thought you were a walking hat."

"My name is Mattie Ross," said I. "The man with the black mark goes by the name of Tom Chaney. He shot my father to death in Fort Smith and robbed him. Chaney was drunk and my father was not armed at the time."

"That is a shame," said the captain.

"When we find him we are going to club him with sticks and put him under arrest and take him back to Fort Smith," said I.

"I wish you luck. We don't want him down here."

Rooster said, "Boots, I need a little help. I have got Haze and some youngster out there, along with Emmett Quincy and Moon Garrett. I am after being in a hurry and I wanted to see if you would not bury them boys for me."

"They are dead?"

"All dead," said Rooster. "What is it the judge says? Their depredations is now come to a fitting end."

Captain Finch pulled the barber's cloth from his neck. He and the barber went with us back to where the horses were tied. Rooster told them about our scrap at the dugout.

The captain grasped each dead man by the hair of the head and when he recognized a face he grunted and spoke the name. The man Haze had no hair to speak of and Captain Finch lifted his head by the ears. We learned that the boy was called Billy. His father ran a steam sawmill on the South Canadian River, the captain told us, and there was a large family at home. Billy was one of the eldest children and he had helped his father cut timber. The boy was not known to have been in any devilment before this. As for the other three, the captain did not know if they had any people who would want to claim the bodies.

Rooster said, "All right, you hold Billy for the family and bury these others. I will post their names in Fort Smith and if anybody wants them they can come dig them up." Then he went along behind the horses slapping their rumps. He said, "These four horses was taken from Mr. Burlingame. These three right here belong to Haze and Quincy and Moon. You get what you can for them, Boots, and sell the saddles and guns and coats and I will split it with you. Is that fair enough?"

I said, "You told Moon you would send his brother the money owing to him from his traps."

Rooster said, "I forgot where he said to send it."

I said, "It is the district superintendent of the

Methodist Church in Austin, Texas. His brother is a preacher named George Garrett."

"Was it Austin or Dallas?"

"Austin."

"Let's get it straight."

"It was Austin."

"All right then, write it down for the captain. Send this man ten dollars, Boots, and tell him his brother got cut and is buried here."

Captain Finch said, "Are you going out by way of Mr. Burlingame's?"

"I don't have the time," said Rooster. "I would like for you to send word out if you will. Just so Mr. Burlingame knows it was deputy marshal Rooster Cogburn that recovered them horses."

"Do you want this girl with the hat to write it down?"

"I believe you can remember it if you try."

Captain Finch called out to some Indian youths who were standing nearby looking at us. I gathered he was telling them in the Choctaw tongue to see to the horses and the burial of the bodies. He had to speak to them a second time and very sharply before they would approach the bodies.

The railroad agent was an older man named Smallwood. He praised us for our pluck and he was very much pleased to see the sacks of cash and valuables we had recovered. You may think Rooster was hard in appropriating the traps of the dead men but I will tell you that he did not touch one cent of the money that was stolen at gunpoint from the passengers of the Katy Flyer. Smallwood looked over the "booty" and said it would certainly help to cover the loss, though it was his experience that some of the victims would make exaggerated claims.

He had known the martyred clerk personally and he said the man had been a loyal employee of the M. K. & T. for some years. In his youth the clerk had been a well-known foot racer in Kansas. He showed his spunk right to the end. Smallwood did not know the fireman personally. In both cases, said he, the M. K. & T. would try to do something for the bereaved families, though times were hard and revenue down. They say Jay Gould had no heart! Smallwood also assured Rooster that the railroad would do right by him, providing he "clean up" Lucky Ned Pepper's robber band and recover the stolen express funds.

I advised Rooster to get a written statement from Smallwood to that effect, along with an itemized, timed and dated receipt for the two sacks of "booty." Smallwood was wary about committing his company too far but we got a receipt out of him and a statement saying that Rooster had produced on that day the lifeless bodies of two men "whom he alleges took part in said robbery." I think Smallwood was a gentleman but gentlemen are only human and their memories can sometimes fail them. Business is business.

Mr. McAlester, who kept the store, was a good Arkansas man. He too commended us for our actions and he gave us towels and pans of hot water and some sweet-smelling olive soap. His wife served us a good country dinner with fresh buttermilk. LaBoeuf joined us for the hearty meal. The medical-trained Indian had been able to remove all the big splinters and lead fragments and he had bound the arm tightly. Naturally the limb remained stiff and sore, yet the Texan enjoyed a limited use of it.

When we had eaten our fill, Mr. McAlester's wife asked me if I did not wish to lie down on her bed for a nap. I was sorely tempted but I saw through the scheme. I had noticed Rooster talking to her on the sly at the table. I concluded he was trying to get shed of me once again. "Thank you, ma'am, I am not tired," said I. It was the biggest story I have ever told!

We did not leave right away because Rooster found that his horse Bo had dropped a front shoe. We went to a little shed kept by a blacksmith. While waiting there, LaBoeuf repaired the broken stock of his Sharps rifle by wrapping copper wire around it. Rooster hurried the smith along with the shoeing, as he was not disposed to linger in the settlement. He wished to stay ahead of the posse of marshals that he knew was even then scouring the brush for Lucky Ned Pepper and his band.

He said to me, "Sis, the time has come when I

must move fast. It is a hard day's ride to where I am going. You will wait here and Mrs. McAlester will see to your comfort. I will be back tomorrow or the next day with our man."

"No, I am going along," said I.

LaBoeuf said, "She has come this far."

Rooster said, "It is far enough."

I said, "Do you think I am ready to quit when we are so close?"

LaBoeuf said, "There is something in what she says, Cogburn. I think she has done fine myself. She has won her spurs, so to speak. That is just my personal opinion."

Rooster held up his hand and said, "All right, let it go. I have said my piece. We won't have a lot of talk about winning spurs."

We departed the place around noon, traveling east and slightly south. Rooster called the turn when he said "hard riding." That big long-legged Bo just walked away from the two ponies, but the weight began to tell on him after a few miles and Little Blackie and the shaggy pony closed the distance on him ere long. We rode like the very "dickens" for about forty minutes and then stopped and dismounted and walked for a spell, giving the horses a rest. It was while we were walking that a rider came up hallooing and overtook us. We were out on a prairie and we saw him coming for some little distance.

It was Captain Finch, and he brought exciting

news. He told us that shortly after we had left McAlester's, he received word that Odus Wharton had broken from the basement jail in Fort Smith. The escape had taken place early that morning.

Here is what happened. Not long after breakfast two trusty prisoners brought in a barrel of clean sawdust for use in the spittoons of that foul dungeon. It was fairly dark down there and in a moment when the guards were not looking the trusties concealed Wharton and another doomed murderer inside the barrel. Both men were of slight stature and inconsiderable weight. The trusties then carried the two outside and away to freedom. A bold daylight escape in a fat barrel! Some clever "stunt"! The trusties ran off along with the convicted killers and very likely drew good wages for their audacity.

On hearing the news Rooster did not appear angry or in any way perturbed, but only amused. You may wonder why. He had his reasons and among them were these, that Wharton now stood no chance of winning a commutation from President R. B. Hayes, and also that the escape would cause Lawyer Goudy a certain amount of chagrin in Washington city and would no doubt result in a big expense loss for him, as clients who resolve their own problems are apt to be slow in paying due bills from a lawyer.

Captain Finch said, "I thought you had better know about this."

Rooster said, "I appreciate it, Boots. I appreciate you riding out here."

"Wharton will be looking for you."

"If he is not careful he will find me."

Captain Finch looked LaBoeuf over, then said to Rooster, "Is this the man who shot Ned's horse from under him?"

Rooster said, "Yes, this is the famous horse killer from El Paso, Texas. His idea is to put everybody on foot. He says it will limit their mischief."

LaBoeuf's fair-complected face became congested with angry blood. He said, "There was very little light and I was firing off-hand. I did not have the time to find a rest."

Captain Finch said, "There is no need to apologize for that shot. A good many more people have missed Ned than have hit him."

"I was not apologizing," said LaBoeuf. "I was only explaining the circumstances."

"Rooster here has missed Ned a few times himself, horse and all," said the captain. "I reckon he is on his way now to missing him again."

Rooster was holding a bottle with a little whiskey in it. He said, "You keep on thinking that." He drained off the whiskey in about three swallows and tapped the cork back in and tossed the bottle up in the air. He pulled his revolver and fired at it twice and missed. The bottle fell and rolled and Rooster shot at it two or three more times and broke it on the ground. He got out his sack of cartridges and reloaded the pistol. He said, "The Chinaman is running them cheap shells in on me again."

LaBoeuf said, "I thought maybe the sun was in your eyes. That is to say, your eye."

Rooster swung the cylinder back in his revolver and said, "Eyes, is it? I'll show you eyes!" He jerked the sack of corn dodgers free from his saddle baggage. He got one of the dodgers out and flung it in the air and fired at it and missed. Then he flung another one up and he hit it. The corn dodger exploded. He was pleased with himself and he got a fresh bottle of whiskey from his baggage and treated himself to a drink.

LaBoeuf pulled one of his revolvers and got two dodgers out of the sack and tossed them both up. He fired very rapidly but he only hit one. Captain Finch tried it with two and missed both of them. Then he tried with one and made a successful shot. Rooster shot at two and hit one. They drank whiskey and used up about sixty corn dodgers like that. None of them ever hit two at one throw with a revolver but Captain Finch finally did it with his Winchester repeating rifle, with somebody else throwing. It was entertaining for a while but there was nothing educational about it. I grew more and more impatient with them.

I said, "Come on, I have had my bait of this. I am ready to go. Shooting cornbread out here on this prairie is not taking us anywhere."

By then Rooster was using his rifle and the captain was throwing for him. "Chunk high and not so far out this time," said he.

At length, Captain Finch took his leave and went back the way he came. We continued our journey eastward, with the Winding Stair Mountains as our destination. We lost a good half-hour with that shooting foolishness, but, worse than that, it started Rooster to drinking.

He drank even as he rode, which looked difficult. I cannot say it slowed him down any but it did make him silly. Why do people *wish* to be silly? We kept up our fast pace, riding hard for forty or fifty minutes and then going on foot for a piece. I believe those walks were a more welcome rest for me than for the horses. I have never claimed to be a cow-boy! Little Blackie did not falter. He had good wind and his spirit was such that he would not let LaBoeuf's shaggy mount get ahead of him on an open run. Yes, you bet he was a game pony!

We loped across open prairies and climbed wooded limestone hills and made our way through brushy bottoms and icy streams. Much of the snow melted under the sun but as the long shadows of dusk descended in all their purple loveliness, the temperature did likewise. We were very warm from our exertions and the chill night air felt good at first, but then it became uncomfortable as we slowed our pace. We did not ride fast after dark as it would have been dangerous for the horses.

LaBoeuf said the Rangers often rode at night to avoid the terrible Texas sun and this was like nothing at all to him. I did not care for it myself.

Nor did I enjoy the slipping and sliding when we were climbing the steep grades of the Winding Stair Mountains. There is a lot of thick pine timber in those hills and we wandered up and down in the double-darkness of the forest. Rooster stopped us twice while he dismounted and looked around for sign. He was well along to being drunk. Later on he got to talking to himself and one thing I heard him say was this: "Well, we done the best we could with what we had. We was in a war. All we had was revolvers and horses." I supposed he was brooding about the hard words LaBoeuf had spoken to him on the subject of his war service. He got louder and louder but it was hard to tell whether he was still talking to himself or addressing himself to us. I think it was a little of both. On one long climb he fell off his horse, but he quickly gained his feet and mounted again.

"That was nothing, nothing," said he. "Bo put a foot wrong, that was all. He is tired. This is no grade. I have freighted iron stoves up harder grades than this, and pork as well. I lost fourteen barrels of pork on a shelf road not much steeper than this and old Cook never batted a eye. I was a pretty fair jerk-line teamster, could always talk to mules, but oxen was something else. You don't get that quick play with cattle that you get with mules.

They are slow to start and slow to turn and slow to stop. It taken me a while to learn it. Pork brought a thundering great price out there then but old Cook was a square dealer and he let me work it out at his lot price. Yes sir, he paid liberal wages too. He made money and he didn't mind his help making money. I will tell you how much he made. He made fifty thousand dollars in one year with them wagons but he did not enjoy good health. Always down with something. He was all bowed over and his neck was stiff from drinking Jamaica ginger. He had to look up at you through his hair, like this, unless he was laying down, and as I say, that rich jaybird was down a lot. He had a good head of brown hair, had every lock until he died. Of course he was a right young man when he died. He only looked old. He was carrying a twenty-one-foot tapeworm along with his business responsibilities and that aged him. Killed him in the end. They didn't even know he had it till he was dead, though he ate like a field hand, ate five or six good dinners every day. If he was alive today I believe I would still be out there. Yes, I know I would, and I would likely have money in the bank. I had to make tracks when his wife commenced to running things. She said, 'You can't leave me like this, Rooster. All my drivers is leaving me,' I told her, I said, 'You watch me.' No sir, I was not ready to work for her and I told her so. There is no generosity in women. They want everything coming in and nothing going out. They show no trust. Lord God, how they hate to pay you! They will get the work of two men out of you and I guess they would beat you with whips if they was able to. No sir, not me. Never. A man will not work for a woman, not unless he has clabber for brains."

LaBoeuf said, "I told you that in Fort Smith."

I do not know if the Texan intended the remark to tell against me, but if he did, it was "water off a duck's back." You cannot give any weight to the words of a drunkard, and even so, I knew Rooster could not be talking about me in his drunken criticism of women, the kind of money I was paying him. I could have confounded him and his silliness right there by saying, "What about me? What about that twenty-five dollars I have given you?" But I had not the strength nor the inclination to bandy words with a drunkard. What have you done when you have bested a fool?

I thought we would never stop, and must be nearing Montgomery, Alabama. From time to time LaBoeuf and I would interrupt Rooster and ask him how much much farther and he would reply, "It is not far now," and then he would pick up again on a chapter in the long and adventurous account of his life. He had seen a good deal of strife in his travels.

When at last we did stop, Rooster said only, "I reckon this will do." It was well after midnight. We were on a more or less level place in a pine forest up in the hills and that was all I could determine. I was so tired and stiff I could not think straight.

Rooster said he calculated we had come about fifty miles—*fifty miles!*—from McAlester's store and were now positioned some four miles from Lucky Ned Pepper's bandit stronghold. Then he wrapped himself up in his buffalo robe and retired without ceremony, leaving LaBoeuf to see to the horses.

The Texan watered them from the canteens and fed them and tied them out. He left the saddles on them for warmth, but with the girths loosened. Those poor horses were worn out.

We made no fire. I took a hasty supper of bacon and biscuit sandwiches. The biscuits were pretty hard. There was a layer of pine straw under the patchy snow and I raked up a thick pile with my hands for a woodland mattress. The straw was dirty and brittle and somewhat damp but at that it made for a better bed than any I had seen on this journey. I rolled up in my blankets and slicker and burrowed down into the straw. It was a clear winter night and I made out the Big Dipper and the North Star through the pine branches. The moon was already down. My back hurt and my feet were swollen and I was so exhausted that my hands quivered. The quivering passed and I was soon in the "land of Nod."

ROOSTER WAS stirring about the next morning before the sun had cleared the higher mountains to the east. He seemed little worse for the wear despite the hard riding and the drinking excesses and the short sleep. He did insist on having coffee and he made a little fire of oak sticks to boil his water. The fire gave off hardly any smoke, white wisps that were quickly gone, but LaBoeuf called it a foolish indulgence, seeing we were so close to our quarry.

I felt as though I had only just closed my eyes. The water in the canteens was low and they would not let me have any for washing. I got the canvas bucket and put my revolver in it and set off down the hill looking for a spring or a runoff stream.

The slope was gentle at first and then it fell off rather sharply. The brush grew thicker and I checked my descent by grabbing bushes. Down and down I went. As I neared the bottom, dreading the return climb, I heard splashing and blowing noises. My thought was: *What on earth!* Then I came into the open on a creek bank. On the other side there was a man watering some horses.

The man was none other than Tom Chaney!

You may readily imagine that I registered shock at the sight of that squat assassin. He had not yet seen me, nor heard me either because of the noise made by the horses. His rifle was slung across his back on the cotton plow line. I thought to turn and run but I could not move. I stood there fixed.

Then he saw me. He gave a start and brought the rifle quickly into play. He held the rifle on me and peered across the little stream and studied me.

He said, "Well, now, I know you. Your name is Mattie. You are little Mattie the bookkeeper. Isn't this something." He grinned and took the rifle from play and slung it carelessly over a shoulder.

I said, "Yes, and I know you, Tom Chaney."

He said, "What are you doing here?"

I said, "I came to fetch water."

"What are you doing here in these mountains?"

I reached into the bucket and brought out my dragoon revolver. I dropped the bucket and held the revolver in both hands. I said, "I am here to take you back to Fort Smith."

Chaney laughed and said, "Well, I will not go. How do you like that?"

I said, "There is a posse of officers up on the hill who will force you to go."

"That is interesting news," said he. "How many is up there?"

"Right around fifty. They are all well armed and they mean business. What I want you to do now is leave those horses and come across the creek and walk in front of me up the hill."

He said, "I think I will oblige the officers to come after me." He began to gather the horses together. There were five of them but Papa's horse Judy was not among them.

I said, "If you refuse to go I will have to shoot you."

He went on with his work and said, "Oh? Then you had better cock your piece."

I had forgotten about that. I pulled the hammer back with both thumbs.

"All the way back till it locks," said Chaney.

"I know how to do it," said I. When it was ready I said, "You will not go with me?"

"I think not," said he. "It is just the other way around. You are going with me."

I pointed the revolver at his belly and shot him down. The explosion kicked me backwards and caused me to lose my footing and the pistol jumped from my hand. I lost no time in recovering it and getting to my feet. The ball had struck Chaney's side and knocked him into a sitting position against a tree. I heard Rooster or LaBoeuf call out for me. "I am down here!" I replied. There was another shout from the hill above Chaney.

He was holding both hands down on his side. He said, "I did not think you would do it."

I said, "What do you think now?"

He said, "One of my short ribs is broken. It hurts every breath I take."

I said, "You killed my father when he was trying to help you. I have one of the gold pieces you took from him. Now give me the other."

"I regret that shooting," said he. "Mr. Ross was decent to me but he ought not to have meddled in my business. I was drinking and I was mad through and through. Nothing has gone right for me."

There was more yelling from the hills.

I said, "No, you are just a piece of trash, that is all. They say you shot a senator in the state of Texas."

"That man threatened my life. I was justified. Everything is against me. Now I am shot by a child."

"Get up on your feet and come across that creek before I shoot you again. My father took you in when you were hungry."

"You will have to help me up."

"No, I will not help you. Get up yourself."

He made a quick move for a chunk of wood and I pulled the trigger and the hammer snapped on a bad percussion cap. I made haste to try another chamber but the hammer snapped dead again. I had not time for a third try. Chaney flung the heavy piece of wood and it caught me in the chest and laid me out backwards.

He came splashing across the creek and he jerked me up by my coat and commenced slapping me and cursing me and my father. That was his cur nature, to change from a whining baby to a vicious bully as circumstances permitted. He stuck my revolver in his belt and pulled me stumbling through the water. The horses were milling about and he managed to catch two of them by their halters while holding me with the other hand.

I heard Rooster and LaBoeuf crashing down through the brush behind us and calling out for me. "Down here! Hurry up!" I shouted, and Chaney let go of my coat just long enough to give me another stinging slap.

I must tell you that the slopes rose steeply on either side of the creek. Just as the two peace officers were running down on one side, so were Chaney's bandit friends running down the other, so that both parties were converging on the hollow and the little mountain stream.

The bandits won the foot race. There were two of them and one was a little man in "woolly chaps" whom I rightly took to be Lucky Ned Pepper. He was still hatless. The other was taller and a quite well-dressed man in a linen suit and a bearskin coat, and his hat tied fast by a slip-string under his chin. This man was the Mexican gambler who called himself The Original Greaser Bob. They broke upon us suddenly and poured a terrible volley of fire across the creek with their Winchester repeating rifles. Lucky Ned Pepper said to Chaney, "Take them horses you got and move!"

Chaney did as he was told and we started up with the horses. It was hard climbing. Lucky Ned Pepper and the Mexican remained behind and exchanged shots with Rooster and LaBoeuf while trying to catch the other horses. I heard running splashes as one of the officers reached the creek, then a flurry of shots as he was made to retreat.

Chaney had to stop and catch his breath after thirty or forty yards of pulling me and the two horses behind him. Blood showed through on his shirt. Lucky Ned Pepper and Greaser Bob overtook us there. They were pulling two horses. I supposed the fifth horse had run away or been killed. The leads of these two horses were turned over to Chaney and Lucky Ned Pepper said to him, "Get on up that hill and don't be stopping again!"

The bandit chieftain took me roughly by the arm. He said, "Who all is down there?"

"Marshal Cogburn and fifty more officers," said I.

He shook me like a terrier shaking a rat. "Tell me another lie and I will stove in your head!" Part of his upper lip was missing, a sort of gap on one side that caused him to make a whistling noise as he spoke. Three or four teeth were broken off there as well, yet he made himself clearly understood.

Thinking it best, I said, "It is Marshal Cogburn and another man."

He flung me to the ground and put a boot on my neck to hold me while he reloaded his rifle from a cartridge belt. He shouted out, "Rooster, can you hear me?" There was no reply. The Original Greaser was standing there with us and he broke the silence by firing down the hill. Lucky Ned Pepper shouted, "You answer me, Rooster! I will kill this girl! You know I will do it!"

Rooster called up from below, "The girl is nothing to me! She is a runaway from Arkansas!"

"That's very well!" said Lucky Ned Pepper. "Do you advise me to kill her?"

"Do what you think is best, Ned!" replied Rooster. "She is nothing to me but a lost child! Think it over first."

"I have already thought it over! You and Potter get mounted double fast! If I see you riding over that bald ridge to the northwest I will spare the girl! You have five minutes!"

"We will need more time!"

"I will not give you any more!"

"There will be a party of marshals in here soon, Ned! Let me have Chaney and the girl and I will mislead them for six hours!"

"Too thin, Rooster! Too thin! I won't trust you!"

"I will cover you till dark!"

"Your five minutes is running! No more talk!"

Lucky Ned Pepper pulled me to my feet. Rooster called up again, saying, "We are leaving but you must give us time!"

The bandit chieftain made no reply. He brushed the snow and dirt from my face and said, "Your life depends upon their actions. I have never busted a cap on a woman or anybody much under sixteen years but I will do what I have to do."

I said, "There is some mix-up here. I am Mattie Ross of near Dardanelle, Arkansas. My family has property and I don't know why I am being treated like this."

Lucky Ned Pepper said, "It is enough that you know I will do what I have to do."

We made our way up the hill. A little farther along we came across a bandit armed with a shotgun and squatting behind a big slab of limestone. This man's name was Harold Permalee. I believe he was simpleminded. He gobbled at me like a turkey until Lucky Ned Pepper made him hush. Greaser Bob was told to stay there with him behind the rock and keep a watch below. I had seen this Mexican gambler fall from Rooster's shots at the dugout but he appeared now to be in perfect health and there was no outward evidence of a wound. When we left them there Harold Permalee made a noise like *"Whooooo-haaaaaaa!"* and this time it was The Greaser who made him hush.

Lucky Ned Pepper pushed me along in front of him through the brush. There was no trail. His woolly chaps sang as they swished back and forth, something like corduroy trousers. He was little and wiry and no doubt a hard customer, but still his wind was not good and he was blowing like a man with asthma by the time we had ascended to the bandits' lair.

They had made their camp on a bare rock shelf some seventy yards or so below the crest of the mountain. Pine timber grew in abundance below and above and on all sides. No apparent trails led to the place.

The ledge was mostly level but broken here and there by deep pits and fissures. A shallow cave provided sleeping quarters, as I saw bedding and saddles strewn about inside. A wagon sheet, now pulled back, served for a door and windbreak. The horses were tied in the cover of trees. It was quite windy up there and the little cooking fire in front of the cave was protected by a circle of rocks. The site overlooked a wide expanse of ground to the west and north.

Tom Chaney was sitting by the fire with his shirt pulled up and another man was ministering to him, tying a pad of cloth to his wounded side with a cotton rope. The man laughed as he cinched the rope up tight and caused Chaney to whimper with pain. "Waw, waw, waw," said the man, making sounds like a bawling calf in mockery of Chaney.

This man was Farrell Permalee, a younger brother to Harold Parmalee. He wore a long blue army overcoat with officers' boards on the shoulders. Harold Parmalee had participated in the robbery of the Katy Flyer and Farrell joined the bandits later that night when they swapped horses at Ma Permalee's place.

The Permalee woman was a notorious receiver of stolen livestock but was never brought to law. Her husband, Henry Joe Permalee, killed himself with a dynamite cap in the ugly act of wrecking a passenger train. A family of criminal trash! Of her youngest boys, Carroll Permalee lived long enough to be put to death in the Electric Chair, and not long afterward Darryl Permalee was shot to death at the wheel of a motorcar by a bank "dick" and a constable in Mena, Arkansas. No, do not compare them to Henry Starr or the Dalton brothers. Certainly Starr and the Daltons were robbers and reckless characters but they were not simple and they were not altogether rotten. You will remember that Bob and Grat Dalton served as marshals for Judge Parker, and Bob was a fine one, they say. Upright men gone bad! What makes them take the wrong road? Bill Doolin too. A cow-boy gone wrong.

When Lucky Ned Pepper and I gained the rock ledge Chaney jumped up and made for me. "I will wring your scrawny neck!" he exclaimed. Lucky Ned Pepper pushed him aside and said, "No, I won't have it. Let that doctoring go and get the horses saddled. Lend him a hand, Farrell."

He pushed me down by the fire and said, "Sit there and be still." When he had caught his breath he took a spyglass from his coat and searched the rocky dome to the west. He saw nothing and took a seat by the fire and drank coffee from a can and ate some bacon from a skillet with his hands. There was plenty of meat and several cans of water in the fire, some with plain water and some with coffee already brewed. I concluded the bandits had been at their breakfast when they were alarmed by the gunshot down below.

I said, "Can I have some of that bacon?"

Lucky Ned Pepper said, "Help yourself. Have some coffee."

"I don't drink coffee. Where is the bread?"

"We lost it. Tell me what you are doing here."

I took a piece of bacon and chewed on it. "I will be glad to tell you," said I. "You will see I am in the right. Tom Chaney there shot my father to death in Fort Smith and robbed him of two gold pieces and stole his mare. Her name is Judy but I do not see her here. I was informed Rooster Cogburn had grit and I hired him out to find the murderer. A few minutes ago I came upon Chaney down there watering horses. He would not be taken in charge and I shot him. If I had killed him I would not now be in this fix. My revolver misfired twice."

"They will do it," said Lucky Ned Pepper. "It will embarrass you every time." Then he laughed. He said, "Most girls like play pretties, but you like guns, don't you?"

"I don't care a thing in the world about guns. If I did I would have one that worked."

Chaney was carrying a load of bedding from the cave. He said, "I was shot from ambush, Ned. The horses was blowing and making noise. It was one of them officers that got me."

I said, "How can you stand there and tell such a big story?"

Chaney picked up a stick and pitched it into a big crack in the ledge. He said, "There is a ball of rattlesnakes down there in that pit and I am going to throw you in it. How do you like that?"

"No, you won't," said I. "This man will not let you have your way. He is your boss and you must do as he tells you."

Lucky Ned Pepper again took his glass and looked across at the ridge.

Chaney said, "Five minutes is well up."

"I will give them a little more time," said the bandit chieftain.

"How much more?" said Chaney.

"Till I think they have had enough."

Greaser Bob called up from below saying, "They are gone, Ned! I can hear nothing! We had best make a move!"

Lucky Ned Pepper replied, "Hold fast for a while!"

Then he returned to his breakfast. He said, "Was that Rooster and Potter that waylaid us last night?"

I said, "The man's name is not Potter, it is LaBoeuf. He is an officer from Texas. He is looking for Chaney too, though he calls him by another name."

"Is he the one with the buffalo gun?"

"He calls it a Sharps rifle. His arm was hurt in the fight."

"He shot my horse. A man from Texas has no authority to fire at me."

"I know nothing about that. I have a good lawyer at home."

"Did they take Quincy and Moon?"

"They are both dead. It was a terrible thing to see. I was in the very middle of it. Do you need a good lawyer?"

"I need a good judge. What about Haze? An old fellow."

"Yes, he and the young man were both killed."

"I saw Billy was dead when he was struck. I thought Haze might have made it. He was tough as boot leather. I am sorry for him."

"Are you not sorry for the boy Billy?"

"He should never have been there. There was nothing I could do for him."

"How did you know he was dead?"

"I could tell. I advised him against coming, and then give in to him against what I knowed was best. Where did you take them?"

"To McAlester's store."

"I will tell you what he did at Wagoner's Switch."

"My lawyer has political influence."

"This will amuse you. I posted him with the horses out of danger and told him to fire a string of shots with his rifle now and then. You must have shooting for the way it keeps the passengers in their seats. Well, he started out all right and then as the job went along I noticed the shots had stopped. I figured Billy Boy had run for home and a plate of mother's soup. Bob went to see about him and he found the boy standing out there in the dark shucking good shells out of his guns. He thought he was shooting but he was so scared he could not remember to pull the trigger. That was how green he was, green as a July persimmon."

I said, "You do not show much kindly feeling for a young man who saved your life."

"I am happy he done it," said Lucky Ned Pepper. "I don't say he wan't game, I say he was green. All kids is game, but a man will keep his head and look out for his own self. Look at old Haze. Well, he is dead now but he should have been dead ten times afore now. Yes, and your good friend Rooster. That goes for him as well."

"He is not my friend."

Farrell Permalee made a whooping noise like that of his brother and said, "There they be!"

I looked over to the northwest and saw two riders approaching the top of the ridge. Little Blackie, riderless, was tied behind them. Lucky Ned Pepper brought his glass into play but I could see them well enough without such aid. When they reached the crest they paused and turned our way and Rooster fired a pistol in the air. I saw the smoke before the noise reached us. Lucky Ned Pepper pulled his revolver and fired an answering shot. Then Rooster and LaBoeuf disappeared over the hill. The last thing I saw was Little Blackie.

I think it did not come home to me until that moment what my situation was. I had not thought Rooster or LaBoeuf would give in to the bandits so easily. It was in my mind that they would slip up through the brush and attack the bandits while they were disorganized, or employ some clever ruse known only by detectives to bring the bandits to heel. Now they were gone! The officers had left me! I was utterly cast down and for the first time I feared for my life. My mind was filled with anxiety.

Who was to blame? *Deputy Marshal Rooster Cogburn!* The gabbing drunken fool had made a mistake of four miles and led us directly into the robbers' lair. A keen detective! Yes, and in an earlier state of drunkenness he had placed faulty caps in my revolver, causing it to fail me in a time of need. That was not enough; now he had abandoned me in this howling wilderness to a gang of cutthroats who cared not a rap for the blood of their own companions, and how much less for that of a helpless and unwanted youngster! Was this what they called grit in Fort Smith? We called it something else in Yell County!

Lucky Ned Pepper shouted out for The Original Greaser and Harold Permalee to leave their watch post and come to the camp. The four horses were saddled and in readiness. Lucky Ned Pepper looked over the mounts, then at the spare saddle that lay on the ground. It was an old saddle but a handsome one, decorated with fixtures of beaten silver.

He said, "That is Bob's saddle."

Tom Chaney said, "It was Bob's horse we lost."

"That you lost," said the bandit chieftain. "Unsaddle that gray and put Bob's saddle up."

"I am riding the gray," said Chaney.

"I have other plans for you."

Chaney set about unsaddling the gray horse. He said, "I will be riding behind Bob?"

"No, it will be too chancy with two men up if it comes to a race. When we reach Ma's house I will send Carroll back to fetch you with a fresh mount. I want you to wait here with the girl. You will be out by dark. We are going to 'The Old Place' and you can meet us there."

"Well, I don't like that," said Chaney. "Let me ride with you, Ned, just out of here anyway."

"No."

"Them marshals will be up here."

"They will guess we are all gone."

I said, "I am not staying here by myself with Tom Chaney."

Lucky Ned Pepper said, "That is the way I will have it."

"He will kill me," said I. "You have heard him say it. He has killed my father and now you will let him kill me."

"He will do no such thing," said the bandit chieftain. "Tom, do you know the crossing at Cypress Forks, near the log meetinghouse?"

"I know the place."

"You will take the girl there and leave her." Then to me, "You can stay the night in the meetinghouse. There is a dummy called Flanagan lives about two miles up the creek. He has a mule and he will see you to McAlester's. He cannot speak or hear but he can read. Can you write?"

"Yes," said I. "Let me go now on foot. I will find my way out."

"No, I won't have it. Tom will not harm you. Do you understand that, Tom? If any harm comes to this child you do not get paid."

Chaney said, "Farrell, let me ride up with you."

Farrell Permalee laughed and made noises like an owl, saying, *"Hoo, hoo, hoo."* Harold Permalee and The Original Greaser Bob came up and Chaney commenced to plead with them to share their mounts. Greaser Bob said no. The Permalee brothers now teamed together like silly boys, and would give Chaney no sensible answer. Harold Permalee would interrupt Chaney's question each time with mockery, making animal sounds such as are made by pigs and goats and sheep, and Farrell would laugh at the sport and say, "Do it again, Harold. Do a goat."

204

Chaney said, "Everything is against me."

Lucky Ned Pepper made sure the buckles were fastened good on his saddle wallets.

Greaser Bob said, "Ned, let us cut up the winnings now."

"There will be time for that at 'The Old Place,'" replied the bandit chieftain.

"We have been in two scraps already," said The Greaser. "We have lost two men. I would feel easier if I was carrying my own winnings."

Lucky Ned Pepper said, "Well, Bob, I thought your interest was in saving time."

"It will not take long. I will feel easier."

"Very well then. It suits me. I want you to feel easy."

He reached inside one of the saddle wallets and pulled out four packets of greenbacks and pitched them to Greaser Bob. "How is that?"

Greaser Bob said, "You will not count it?"

"We won't quarrel over a dollar or two." Then he gave one packet to Harold Permalee and a single fifty-dollar note to Farrell Permalee. The brothers said, *"Whooooo-haaaaa! Whooooo-haaaaa!"* I wondered that they did not press for more, in light of the total amount realized in the robbery, but I supposed they had agreed to a fixed wage for their services. I judged too that they were somewhat ignorant of the value of money.

Lucky Ned Pepper went to buckle up the wallet again. He said, "I will keep your winnings with mine, Tom. You will be paid tonight at 'The Old Place.' "

Chaney said, "Nothing is going right for me."

Greaser Bob said, "What about the registered pouch?"

"Well, and what about it?" said Lucky Ned Pepper. "Are you expecting a letter, Bob?"

"If there is any money in it we may as well have it now. It makes no sense to carry the pouch about for evidence."

"You still don't feel easy?"

"You are making too much of my words, Ned."

Lucky Ned Pepper thought about it. He said, "Well, maybe so." Once more he unbuckled the straps. He took out a locked canvas bag and cut it open with a Barlow knife and dumped the contents on the ground. He grinned and said, "Christmas gift!" Of course that is what children shout to one another early on Christmas morning, the game being to shout it first. I had not thought before of this disfigured robber having had a childhood. I expect he was mean to cats and made rude noises in church when he was not asleep. When he needed a firm restraining hand, it was not there. An old story!

There were only six or seven pieces of mail in the bag. There were some personal letters, one with twenty dollars in it, and some documents that appeared to be of a legal description, such as contracts. Lucky Ned Pepper glanced at them and flung them away. A bulky gray envelope tied with ribbon held a packet of one hundred twenty-dollar notes on the Whelper Commercial Bank of Denison, Texas. Another envelope held a check.

Lucky Ned Pepper studied it, then said to me, "Do you read well?"

"I read very well," said I.

He passed over the check. "Is this any good to me?"

It was a cashier's check for twenty-seven hundred fifty dollars drawn on the Grangers Trust Company of Topeka, Kansas, to a man named Marshall Purvis. I said, "This is a cashier's check for twenty-seven hundred fifty dollars drawn on the Grangers Trust Company of Topeka, Kansas, to a man named Marshall Purvis."

"I can see what it is worth," said the bandit. "Is it any good?"

"It is good if the bank is good," said I. "But it must be endorsed by this Purvis. The bank guarantees the check account is good."

"What about these notes?"

I looked over the banknotes. They were brand-new. I said, "They are not signed. They are no good unless they are signed."

"Can you not sign them?"

"They must be signed by Mr. Whelper, the president of the bank."

"Is it such a hard name to spell?"

"It is an unusual name but it is not hard to spell. The name is printed right here. That is his signature, the printed signature of Monroe G. B. Whelper, the president of the Whelper Commercial Bank of Denison, Texas. That signature must be matched over here."

"I want you to sign them. And this check too."

Naturally I did not wish to use my education in this robber's service and I hesitated.

He said, "I will box your ears until your head rings."

I said, "I have nothing to write with."

He drew a cartridge from his belt and opened his Barlow knife again. "This will answer. I will shave the lead down."

"They must be signed in ink."

Greaser Bob said, "We can attend to it later, Ned. This matter will keep."

"We will attend to it now," replied the bandit chieftain. "You are the one who wanted to look at the mail. This paper is worth over four thousand dollars with a little writing. The girl can write. Harold, go to the trash pile and fetch me a good stout turkey feather, a dry one, a big tail feather." Then he pulled the bullet out of the cartridge case with his snag teeth and poured the black powder in the palm of his hand. He spit on it through the gap and stirred the glutinous mess about with a finger.

Harold Permalee brought back a handful of feathers and Lucky Ned Pepper chose one and cut the tip off with his knife and reamed out the hole a little. He dipped the quill into the "ink" and printed

NED on his wrist in childish characters. He said, "There. You see. That is my name. Is it not?"

I said, "Yes, that is *Ned*."

He handed me the feather. "Now go to it."

A flat rock with one of the contracts laid on it was made to serve for a desk. It is not in me to do poor work where writing is concerned and I toiled earnestly at making faithful copies of Mr. Whelper's signature. However, the makeshift pen and ink were not satisfactory. The writing jumped and spread wide and pinched thin. It looked as though it had been done with a stick. My thought was: *Who will believe that Mr. Whelper signs his banknotes with a stick?*

But the unlettered bandit chieftain knew little of the world of banking except for such glimpses as he got over a gun sight, and he was pleased with the work. I signed and signed, using his palm for an inkwell. It was very tiring. As soon as I had finished one note he would snatch it up and pass me another.

He said, "They are as good as gold, Bob. I will trade them at Colbert's."

Greaser Bob said, "Nothing on paper is as good as gold. That is my belief."

"Well, that is how much a damned Mexican knows."

"It is every man to his own principles. Tell her to hurry along."

When the criminal task was completed Lucky

Ned Pepper put the notes and the check in the gray envelope and secured it in his saddle wallet. He said, "Tom, we will see you tonight. Make yourself agreeable to this child. Little Carroll will be here before you know it."

Then they departed the place, not riding their horses but leading them, as the hill was so steep and brushy.

I was alone with Tom Chaney!

He sat across the fire from me, my pistol in his waistband and the Henry rifle in his lap. His face was a "brown study." I stirred up the fire a little and arranged some glowing coals around one of the cans of hot water.

Chaney watched me. He said, "What are you doing?"

I said, "I am heating some water so that I may wash this black off my hands."

"A little smut will not harm you."

"Yes, that is true, or else you and your 'chums' would surely be dead. I know it will not harm me but I would rather have it off."

"Don't provoke me. You will find yourself in that pit."

"Lucky Ned Pepper has warned you that if you molest me in any way he will not pay you. He means business too."

"I fear he has no idea of paying me. I believe he has left me, knowing I am sure to be caught when I leave on foot."

"He promised he would meet you at 'The Old Place.'"

"Keep still. I must now think over my position and how I may improve it."

"What about my position? At least you have not been abandoned by a man who was paid and pledged to protect you."

"You little busybody! What does your kind know of hardship and affliction? Now keep still while I think."

"Are you thinking about 'The Old Place'?"

"No, I am not thinking about 'The Old Place.' Carroll Permalee or nobody else is coming up here with any horse. They are not going to 'The Old Place.' I am not so easily fooled as some people might think."

I thought to ask him about the other gold piece, then checked myself, afraid that he might force me to give over the one I had recovered. I said, "What have you done with Papa's mare?"

He gave no answer.

I said, "If you will let me go now I will keep silent as to your whereabouts for two days."

"I tell you I can do better than that," said he. "I can have your silence forever. I will not tell you again to hold your tongue."

The water was not boiling but it had begun to steam a little and I picked up the can with a rag and flung it at him, then took to my feet in frantic flight. Though caught by surprise, he managed to shield his face with his arms. He yelped and gave immediate pursuit. My desperate plan was to reach the trees. Once there, I thought to evade him and finally lose him by darting this way and that in the brush.

It was not to be! Just as I came to the edge of the rock shelf, Chaney grabbed my coat from behind and pulled me up short. My thought was: *I am certainly done for!* Chaney was cursing me and he struck me on the head with the pistol barrel. The blow made me see stars and I concluded I was shot, not knowing the sensation caused by a bullet striking your head. My thoughts turned to my peaceful home in Arkansas, and my poor mother who would be laid low by the news. First her husband and now her oldest child, both gone in the space of two weeks and dispatched by the same bloody hand! That was the direction of my thoughts.

Suddenly I heard a familiar voice, and the words were hard with authority. "Hands up, Chelmsford! Move quickly! It is all up with you! Have a care with that pistol!"

It was LaBoeuf the Texan! He had come up the back way, on foot I supposed, as he was panting for breath. He was standing not thirty feet away with his wired-together rifle trained on Chaney.

Chaney let go of my coat and dropped the pistol.

"Everything is against me," he said. I recovered the pistol.

LaBoeuf said, "Are you hurt, Mattie?"

"I have a painful knot on my head," said I.

He said to Chaney, "I see you are bleeding."

"It was this girl done it," said he. "I am shot in the ribs and bleeding again. It hurts when I cough."

I said, "Where is Rooster?"

LaBoeuf said, "He is down below watching the front door. Let us find a place where we can see. Move with care, Chelmsford!"

We proceeded to the northwest corner of the rock shelf, skirting around the pit which had figured in Chaney's ugly threats. "Watch your step there," I cautioned the Texan. "Tom Chaney says there are deadly snakes at the bottom having their winter sleep."

From the far corner of the ledge we had a clear prospect. The timbered slope dropped off sharply below us and led to a meadow. This meadow, level and open, was quite high itself and at the other end there was a further descent leading down out of the Winding Stair Mountains.

No sooner had we taken up our vigil than we were rewarded with the sight of Lucky Ned Pepper and the other three bandits emerging from the trees into the meadow. There they mounted their horses and headed them west, away from us. They had hardly started their ride when a lone horseman came out of the brush at the western end of the field. The horse was walking and the rider took him out to the middle of the open space and stopped, so as to block the passage of the four desperadoes.

Yes, it was Rooster Cogburn! The bandits checked up and faced him from some seventy or eighty yards' distance. Rooster had one of the navy revolvers in his left hand and he held the reins in his right hand. He said, "Where is the girl, Ned?"

Lucky Ned Pepper said, "She was in wonderful health when last I saw her! I cannot answer for her now!"

"You will answer for her now!" said Rooster. "Where is she?"

LaBoeuf stood up and cupped his hands and shouted down, "She is all right, Cogburn! I have Chelmsford as well! Make a run for it!" I confirmed the news by shouting, "I am fine, Rooster! We have Chaney! You must get away!"

The bandits turned to look up at us and no doubt they were surprised and not a little disconcerted by the interesting development. Rooster made no reply to us and gave no sign of leaving the place.

Lucky Ned Pepper said, "Well, Rooster, will you give us the road? We have business elsewhere!"

Rooster said, "Harold, I want you and your brother to stand clear! I have no interest in you today! Stand clear now and you will not be hurt!"

Harold Permalee's answer was to crow like a rooster, and the *"Cock-a-doodle-doo!"* brought a hearty laugh from his brother Farrell.

Lucky Ned Pepper said, "What is your intention? Do you think one on four is a dogfall?"

Rooster said, "I mean to kill you in one minute, Ned, or see you hanged in Fort Smith at Judge Parker's convenience! Which will you have?"

Lucky Ned Pepper laughed. He said, "I call that bold talk for a one-eyed fat man!"

Rooster said, "Fill your hand, you son of a bitch!" and he took the reins in his teeth and pulled the other saddle revolver and drove his spurs into the flanks of his strong horse Bo and charged directly at the bandits. It was a sight to see. He held the revolvers wide on either side of the head of his plunging steed. The four bandits accepted the challenge and they likewise pulled their arms and charged their ponies ahead.

It was some daring move on the part of the deputy marshal whose manliness and grit I had doubted. No grit? Rooster Cogburn? *Not much!*

LaBoeuf instinctively brought his rifle up, but then he relaxed it and did not fire. I pulled at his coat, saying, "Shoot them!" The Texan said, "They are too far and they are moving too fast."

I believe the bandits began firing their weapons first, although the din and smoke was of such a sudden, general nature that I cannot be sure. I do know that the marshal rode for them in so determined and unwavering a course that the bandits broke their "line" where he reached them and raced through them, his revolvers blazing, and he not aiming with the sights but only pointing the barrels and snapping his head from side to side to bring his good eye into play.

Harold Permalee was the first to go down. He flung his shotgun in the air and clutched at his neck and was thrown backward over the rump of his horse. The Original Greaser Bob rode wider than the others and he lay flat on his horse and escaped clear with his winnings. Farrell Permalee was hit and a moment later his horse went down with a broken leg and Farrell was dashed violently forward to his death.

We thought that Rooster had come through the ordeal with no injury, but in fact he had caught several shotgun pellets in his face and shoulders, and his horse Bo was mortally struck. When Rooster attempted to rein up with his teeth and turn to resume the attack, the big horse fell to the side and Rooster under him.

The field now remained to one rider and that was Lucky Ned Pepper. He wheeled his horse about. His left arm hung limp and useless, but he yet held a revolver in his right hand. He said, "Well, Rooster, I am shot to pieces!" Rooster had lost his big revolvers in the fall and he was struggling to pull his belt gun which was trapped to the ground under the weight of horse and rider.

Lucky Ned Pepper nudged his pony forward in a trot and he bore down on the helpless officer.

LaBoeuf quickly stirred beside me and assumed

a sitting position with the Sharps rifle, his elbows locked against his knees. He took only a second to draw a bead and fire the powerful gun. The ball flew to its mark like a martin to his gourd and Lucky Ned Pepper fell dead in the saddle. The horse reared and the body of the bandit was thrown clear and the horse fled in panic. The distance covered by LaBoeuf's wonderful shot at the moving rider was over six hundred yards. I am prepared to swear an affidavit to it.

"Hurrah!" I joyfully exclaimed. "Hurrah for the man from Texas! Some bully shot!" LaBoeuf was pleased with himself and he reloaded his rifle.

Now the prisoner has an advantage over his keeper in this respect, that he is always thinking of escape and watching for opportunities, while the keeper does not constantly think of keeping him. Once his man is subdued, so the guard believes, little else is needed but the presence and threat of superior force. He thinks of happy things and allows his mind to wander. It is only natural. Were it otherwise, the keeper would be a prisoner of the prisoner.

So it was that LaBoeuf (and I too) was distracted for a dangerous moment in appreciation of the timely rifle shot that saved Rooster Cogburn's life. Tom Chaney, seizing the occasion, picked up a rock about the size of a new cooking pumpkin and broke LaBoeuf's head with it.

The Texan fell over with a groan of agony. I

screamed and hastened to my feet and backed away, bringing my pistol to bear once again on Tom Chaney, who was scrambling after the Sharps rifle. Would the old dragoon revolver fail me this time? I hoped it would not.

I hurriedly cocked the hammer and pulled the trigger. The charge exploded and sent a lead ball of justice, too long delayed, into the criminal head of Tom Chaney.

Yet I was not to taste the victory. The kick of the big pistol sent me reeling backward. I had forgotten about the *pit* behind me! Over the edge I went, then tumbling and bouncing against the irregular sides, and all the while I was grabbing wildly for something and finding nothing. I struck the bottom with a thump that fairly dazed me. The wind was knocked from my lungs and I lay still for a moment until I had regained my breath. I was addled and I had the fanciful notion that my spirit was floating out of my body, escaping through my mouth and nostrils.

I had thought myself to be lying down, but when I made to get up I found I was stuck upright in a small hole, the lower part of my body wedged in tight between mossy rocks. I was caught like a cork in a bottle!

My right arm was pinned against my side and I could not pull it free. When I tried to use my left hand to push myself out of the hole I saw with a shock that the forearm was bent in an unnatural attitude. The arm was broken! There was little pain in the arm, only a kind of "pins and needles" numbness. The movement in my fingers was weak and I had but little grasping power. I was reluctant to use the arm for leverage, fearing the pressure would worsen the fracture and bring on pain.

It was cold and dark down there, though not totally dark. A slender column of sunshine came down from above and ended in a small pool of light some three or four feet away on the stone floor of the cavern. I looked up at the column and could see floating particles of dust stirred up by my fall.

I saw on the rocks about me a few sticks and bits of paper and an old tobacco sack and splotches of grease where skillets had been emptied. I also saw the corner of a man's blue cotton shirt, the rest of it being obscured by shadow. There were no snakes about. Thank goodness for that!

I summoned my strength and cried out, "Help! LaBoeuf! Can you hear me!" No word of reply came. I did not know if the Texan were alive or dead. All I heard was a low roaring of the wind above and dripping noises behind me and some faint "cheeps" and "squeaks." I could not identify the nature of the squeaks or locate their origin.

I renewed my effort to break free but the vigorous movement made me slip a bit farther down in the mossy hole. My thought was: *This will not do.* I stopped maneuvering lest I drop right through the hole to what depths of blackness I could only imagine. My legs swung free below and my jeans were bunched up so that portions of bare leg were exposed. I felt something brush against one of my legs and I thought, *Spider!* I kicked and flailed my feet and then I stopped when my body settled downward another inch or so.

Now more squeaks, and it came to me that there were *bats* in the cavern below. *Bats* were making the noise and it had been a *bat* that attached himself to my leg. Yes, I had disturbed them. Their roosting place was below. This hole I now so effectively plugged was their opening to the outside.

I had no unreasonable fear of bats, knowing them for timid little creatures, yet I knew them too for carriers of the dread "Hydrophobia," for which there was no specific. What would the bats do, come night and their time to fly, and they found their opening to the outer world closed off? Would they bite? If I struggled and kicked against them I would surely shake myself through the hole. But I knew I had not the will to remain motionless and let them bite.

Night! Was I to be here then till night? I must keep my head and guard against such thoughts. What of LaBoeuf? And what had become of Rooster Cogburn? He had not appeared to be badly hurt in the fall of his horse. But how would he know I was down here? I did not like my situation.

I thought to set fire to bits of cloth for a signal of smoke but the idea was useless because I had no matches. Surely someone would come. Perhaps Captain Finch. The news of the gun fight must get out and bring a party to investigate. Yes, the posse of marshals. The thing was to hold tight. Help was sure to come. At least there were no snakes. I settled on this course: I would give cries for help every five minutes or as near on that interval as I could guess it to be.

I called out at once and was again mocked by the echo of my own voice and by the wind and the dripping of the cave water and the squeaking of the bats. I told numbers to measure the time. It occupied my mind and gave me a sense of purpose and method.

I had not counted far when my body slipped down appreciably and with panic in my breast I realized that the moss which gripped me in a tight seal was tearing loose. I looked about for something to hold to, broken arm or not, but my hand found only slick and featureless planes of rock. I was going through. It was a matter now of time.

Another lurch down, to the level of my right elbow. That bony knob served as a momentary check but I could feel the moss giving way against it. A wedge! That was what I needed. Something to stuff in the hole with me to make the cork fit more snugly. Or a long stick to pass under my arm.

I cast my eyes about for something suitable. The few sticks lying about were none of them long enough or stout enough for my purpose. If only I could reach the blue shirt! It would be just the thing for packing. I broke one stick scratching and pulling at the shirttail. With the second one I managed to bring it within reach of my fingertips. Weakened as my hand was, I got a purchase on the cloth with thumb and finger and pulled it out of the dark. It was unexpectedly heavy. Something was attached to it.

Suddenly I jerked my hand away as though from a hot stove. The *something* was the corpse of a man! Or more properly, a skeleton. He was wearing the shirt. I did nothing for a minute, so frightful and astonishing was the discovery. I could see a good part of the remains, the head with patches of bright orange hair showing under a piece of rotted black hat, one shirtsleeved arm and that portion of the trunk from about the waist upwards. The shirt was buttoned in two or three places near the neck.

I soon recovered my wits. *I am falling. I need that shirt.* These thoughts bore upon me with urgency. I had no stomach for the task ahead but there was nothing else to be done in my desperate circumstances. My plan was to give the shirt a smart jerk in hopes of tearing it free from the skeleton. *I will have that shirt!*

Thus I took hold of the garment again and snatched it toward me with such sharp force as I could muster. My arm seized up with a stab of pain and I let go. After a little tingling the pain subsided and gave way to a dull and tolerable ache. I examined the result of my effort. The buttons had torn free and now the body was within reach. The shirt itself remained clothed about the shoulders and arm bones in a careless fashion. I saw too that the maneuver had exposed the poor man's rib cage.

One more pull and I would have the body close enough so that I could work the shirt free. As I made ready for the job my eyes were attracted to something—movement?—within the cavity formed by the curving gray ribs. I leaned over for a closer look. *Snakes! A ball of snakes!* I flung myself back but of course there was no real retreat for me, imprisoned as I was in the mossy trap.

I cannot accurately guess the number of rattlesnakes in the ball, as some were big, bigger than my arm, and others small, ranging down to the size of lead pencils, but I believe there were not fewer than forty. With trembling heart I looked on as they writhed sluggishly about in the man's chest. I had disturbed their sleep in their curious winter quarters and now, more or less conscious, they had begun to move and detach themselves from the tangle, falling this way and that.

This, thought I, is a pretty fix. I desperately needed the shirt but I did not wish to "mess" further with the snakes in order to have it. Even while I considered these things I was settling and being drawn down to . . . *what?* Perhaps a black and bottomless pool of water where the fish were white and had no eyes to see.

I wondered if the snakes could bite in their present lethargic state. I thought they could not see well, if at all, but I observed too that the light and warmth of the sun had an invigorating effect on them. We kept two speckled king snakes in our corn crib to eat rats and I was not afraid of them, Saul and Little David, but I really knew nothing about snakes. Moccasins and rattlers were to be avoided if possible and killed if there was a chopping hoe handy. That was all I knew about poisonous snakes.

The ache in my broken arm grew worse. I felt some more of the binding moss give way against my right arm and at the same time I saw that some of the snakes were crawling out through the man's ribs. *Lord help me!*

I set my teeth and took hold of the bony hand that stuck forth from the blue shirtsleeve. I gave a yank and pulled the man's arm clean away from the shoulder. A terrible thing to do, you say, but you will see that I now had something to work with.

I studied the arm. Bits of cartilage held it together at the elbow joint. With some twisting I managed to separate it at that place. I took the long bone of the upper arm and secured it under my armpit to serve as a cross-member. This would keep me from plunging through the hole should I reach that point in my descent. It was quite a long bone and, I hoped, a strong one. I was grateful to the poor man for being tall.

What I had left now was the lower part, the two bones of the forearm, and the hand and wrist, all of a piece. I grasped it at the elbow and proceeded to use it as a flail to keep the snakes at bay. "Here, get away!" said I, slapping at them with the bony hand. "Get back, you!" This was well enough except that I perceived the agitation only caused them to be more active. In trying to keep them away, I was at the same time stirring them up! They moved very slowly but there were so many I could not keep track of them all.

Each blow I struck brought burning pain to my arm and you can imagine these blows were not hard enough to kill the snakes. That was not my idea. My idea was to keep them back and prevent them from getting behind me. My striking range from left to right was something short of one hundred eighty degrees and I knew if the rattlers got behind me I would be in a fine "pickle."

I heard noises above. A shower of sand and pebbles came cascading down. "Help!" I cried out. "I am down here! I need help!" My thought was: *Thank God. Someone has come. Soon I will be out of this hellish place.* I saw drops of something spattering on a rock in front of me. It was blood. "Hurry up!" I yelled. "There are snakes and skeletons down here!"

A man's voice called down, saying, "I warrant there will be another one before spring! A little spindly one!"

It was the voice of Tom Chaney! I had not yet made a good job of killing him! I supposed he was leaning over the edge and the blood was falling from his wounded head.

"How do you like it?" he taunted.

"Throw me a rope, Tom! You cannot be mean enough to leave me!"

"You say you don't like it?"

Then I heard a shout and the sounds of a scuffle and a dreadful crunch, which was Rooster Cogburn's rifle stock smashing the wounded head of Tom Chaney. There followed a furious rush of rocks and dust. The light was blocked off and I made out a large object hurtling down toward me. It was the body of Tom Chaney. I leaned back as far as I could to avoid being struck, and at that it was a near thing.

He fell directly upon the skeleton, crushing the bones and filling my face and eyes with dirt and scattering the puzzled rattlesnakes every which way. They were all about me and I commenced striking at them with such abandon that my body dropped free through the hole. *Gone!*

No! Checked short! I was shakily suspended in space by the bone under my armpit. Bats flew up past my face and the ones below were carrying on like a treefull of sparrows at sundown. Only my head and my left arm and shoulder now remained above the hole. I hung at an uncomfortable angle. The bone was bowed under my weight and I prayed it would hold. My left arm was cramped and fully occupied in holding to it and I had not the use of the hand in fending off the snakes.

"Help!" I called. "I need help!"

Rooster's voice came booming down, saying, "Are you all right?"

"No! I am in a bad way! Hurry up!"

"I am pitching down a rope! Fasten it under your arms and tie it with a good knot!"

"I cannot manage a rope! You will have to come down and help me! Hurry up, I am falling! There are snakes all about my head!"

"Hold on! Hold on!" came another voice. It was LaBoeuf. The Texan had survived the blow. The officers were both safe.

I watched as two rattlers struck and sunk their sharp teeth into Tom Chaney's face and neck. The body was lifeless and made no protest. My thought was: *Those scoundrels can bite in December and right there is the proof of it!* One of the smaller snakes approached my hand and rubbed his nose against it. I moved my hand a little and the snake moved to it and touched his nose to the flesh again.

He moved a bit more and commenced to rub the underside of his jaw on top of my hand.

From the corner of my eye I saw another snake on my left shoulder. He was motionless and limp. I could not tell if he was dead or merely asleep. Whatever the case, I did not want him there and I began to swing my body gently from side to side on the bone axle. The movement caused the serpent to roll over with his white belly up and I gave my shoulder a shake and he fell into the darkness below.

I felt a sting and I saw the little snake pulling his head away from my hand, an amber drop of venom on his mouth. He had bitten me. The hand was already well along to being dead numb from the cramped position and I hardly felt it. It was on the order of a horsefly bite. I counted myself lucky the snake was small. That was how much I knew of natural history. People who know tell me the younger snakes carry the more potent poison, and that it weakens with age. I believe what they say.

Now here came Rooster with a rope looped around his waist and his feet against the sides of the pit, descending in great violent leaps and sending another shower of rocks and dust down on me. He landed with a heavy bump and then it seemed he was doing everything at once. He grasped the collar of my coat and shirt behind my neck and heaved me up from the hole with one hand, at the same time kicking at snakes and shooting them with his belt revolver. The noise was deafening and made my head ache.

My legs were wobbly. I could hardly stand.

Rooster said, "Can you hold to my neck?"

I said, "Yes, I will try." There were two dark red holes in his face with dried rivulets of blood under them where shotgun pellets had struck him.

He stooped down and I wrapped my right arm around his neck and lay against his back. He tried to climb the rope hand over hand with his feet against the sides of the pit but he made only about three pulls and had to drop back down. Our combined weight was too much for him. His right shoulder was torn from a bullet too, although I did not know it at the time.

"Stay behind me!" he said, kicking and stomping the snakes while he reloaded his pistol. A big grandfather snake coiled himself around Rooster's boot and got his head shot off for his boldness.

Rooster said, "Do you think you can climb the rope?"

"My arm is broken," said I. "And I am bit on the hand."

He looked at the hand and pulled his dirk knife and cut the place to scarify it. He squeezed blood from it and took some smoking tobacco and hurriedly chewed it into a cud and rubbed it over the wound to draw the poison.

Then he harnessed the rope tightly under my arms. He shouted up to the Texan, saying, "Take the rope, LaBoeuf! Mattie is hurt! I want you to pull her up in easy stages! Can you hear me?"

LaBoeuf replied, "I will do what I can!"

The rope grew taut and lifted me to my toes. "Pull!" shouted Rooster. "The girl is snake-bit, man! Pull!" But LaBoeuf could not do it, weakened as he was by his bad arm and broken head. "It's no use!" he said. "I will try the horse!"

In a matter of minutes he had fastened the rope to a pony. "I am ready!" the Texan called down to us. "Take a good hold!"

"Go!" said Rooster.

He had looped the rope about his hips and once around his waist. He held me with the other arm. We were jerked from our feet. Now there was power at the other end! We went up in bounds. Rooster worked to keep us clear of the rough sides with his feet. We were skinned up a little.

Sunlight and blue sky! I was so weak that I lay upon the ground and could not speak. I blinked my eyes to accommodate them to the brightness and I saw that LaBoeuf was sitting with his bloody head in his hands and gasping from his labors in driving the horse. Then I saw the horse. It was Little Blackie! The scrub pony had saved us! My thought was: *The stone which the builders rejected, the same is become the head of the corner.*

Rooster tied the cud of tobacco on top of my hand with a rag. He said, "Can you walk?"

"Yes, I think so," said I. He led me toward the

horse and when I had walked a few steps I was overcome with nausea and I dropped to my knees. When the sickness had passed, Rooster helped me along and placed me in the saddle astride Little Blackie. He bound my feet to the stirrups and with another length of rope he tied my waist to the saddle, front and back. Then he mounted behind me.

He said to LaBoeuf, "I will send help as soon as I can. Don't wander off."

I said, "We are not leaving him?"

Rooster said, "I must get you to a doctor, sis, or you are not going to make it." He said to LaBoeuf as an afterthought, "I am in your debt for that shot, pard."

The Texan said nothing and we left him there holding his head. I expect he was feeling pretty bad. Rooster spurred Blackie away and the faithful pony stumbled and skidded down the steep and brushy hill where prudent horsemen led their mounts. The descent was dangerous and particularly so with such a heavy burden as Blackie was carrying. There was no way to dodge all the limbs. Rooster lost his hat and never looked back.

We galloped across the meadow where the smoky duel had lately occurred. My eyes were congested from nausea and through a tearful haze I saw the dead horses and the bodies of the bandits. The pain in my arm became intense and I commenced to cry and the tears were blown back in streams around my cheeks. Once down from the mountains we headed north, and I guessed we were aiming for Fort Smith. Despite the load, Blackie held his head high and ran like the wind, perhaps sensing the urgency of the mission. Rooster spurred and whipped him without let. I soon passed away in a faint.

When I regained my senses, I realized we had slowed. Heaving and choking for breath, Blackie was yet giving us all he had. I cannot say how many miles we had ridden full out. Poor lathered beast! Rooster whipped and whipped.

"Stop!" I said. "We must stop! He is played out!" Rooster paid me no heed. Blackie was all in and as he stumbled and made to stop, Rooster took his dirk knife and cut a brutal slash on the pony's withers. "Stop it! Stop it!" I cried. Little Blackie squealed and burst forth in a run under the stimulation of the pain. I wrestled for the reins but Rooster slapped my hands away. I was crying and yelling. When Blackie slowed again, Rooster took salt from his pocket and rubbed the wound with it and the pony leaped forward as before. In a very few minutes this torture was mercifully ended. Blackie fell to the ground and died, his brave heart burst and mine broken. There never lived a nobler pony.

No sooner were we down than Rooster was cutting me free. He ordered me to climb upon his back. I held fast around his neck with my right arm and he supported my legs with his arms. Now Rooster himself began to run, or jog as it were under the load, and his breath came hard. Once more I lost my senses and the next I knew I was being carried in his arms and sweat drops from his brow and mustache were falling on my neck.

I have no recollection of the stop at the Poteau River where Rooster commandeered a wagon and a team of mules from a party of hunters at gunpoint. I do not mean to suggest the hunters were reluctant to lend their team in such an emergency but Rooster was impatient of explanation and he simply took the rig. Farther along the river we called at the home of a wealthy Indian farmer named Cullen. He provided us with a buggy and a fast span of matched horses, and he also sent one of his sons along mounted on a white pony to lead the way.

Night had fallen when we reached Fort Smith. We rode into town in a drizzle of cold rain. I remember being carried into the home of Dr. J. R. Medill, with Dr. Medill holding his hat over a coal oil lamp to keep the rain off the mantle.

I was in a stupor for days. The broken bone was set and an open splint was fixed along my forearm. My hand swelled and turned black, and then my wrist. On the third day Dr. Medill gave me a sizable dose of morphine and amputated the arm just above the elbow with a little surgical saw. My mother and Lawyer Daggett sat at my side while this work was done. I very much admired my mother for sitting there and not flinching, as she was of a delicate temperament. She held my right hand and wept.

I remained in the doctor's home for something over a week after the operation. Rooster called on me twice but I was so sick and "dopey" that I made poor company. He had patches on his face where Dr. Medill had removed the shotgun balls. He told me the posse of marshals had found LaBoeuf, and that the officer had refused to leave the place until he had recovered the body of Tom Chaney. None of the marshals was anxious to go down in the pit, so LaBoeuf had them lower him on a rope. He did the job, though his vision was somewhat confounded from the blow on his head. At McAlester's he was given such treatment as was available for the depression on his head, and from there he left for Texas with the corpse of the man on whose trail he had camped for so long.

I went home on a varnish train, lying flat on my back on a stretcher that was placed in the aisle of a coach. As I say, I was quite sick and it was not until I had been home for a few days that I fully recovered my faculties. It came to me that I had not paid Rooster the balance of his money. I wrote a check for seventy-five dollars and put it in an envelope and asked Lawyer Daggett to mail it to Rooster in care of the marshal's office.

Lawyer Daggett interviewed me about it and in

the course of our conversation I learned something disturbing. It was this. The lawyer had blamed Rooster for taking me on the search for Tom Chaney and had roundly cursed him and threatened to prosecute him in a court action. I was upset on hearing it. I told Lawyer Daggett that Rooster was in no way to blame, and was rather to be praised and commended for his grit. He had certainly saved my life.

Whatever his adversaries, the railroads and steamboat companies, may have thought, Lawyer Daggett was a gentleman, and on hearing the straight of the matter he was embarrassed by his actions. He said he still considered the deputy marshal had acted with poor judgment, but in the circumstances was deserving an apology. He went to Fort Smith and personally delivered the seventy-five dollars owing to him, and then presented him with a two-hundred-dollar check of his own and asked him to accept his apology for the hard and unfair words he had spoken.

I wrote Rooster a letter and invited him to visit us. He replied with a short note that looked like one of his "vouchers," saying he would try to stop by when next he took prisoners to Little Rock. I concluded he would not come and I made plans to go there when I had the use of my legs. I was very curious to know how much he had realized, if anything, in the way of rewards for his destruction of Lucky Ned Pepper's robber band, and whether he had received news of LaBoeuf. I will say here that Judy was never recovered, nor was the second California gold piece. I kept the other one for years, until our house burned. We found no trace of it in the ashes.

But I never got the chance to visit him. Not three weeks after we had returned from the Winding Stair Mountains, Rooster found himself in trouble over a gun duel he fought in Fort Gibson, Cherokee Nation. He shot and killed Odus Wharton in the duel. Of course Wharton was a convicted murderer and a fugitive from the gallows but there was a stir about the manner of the shooting. Rooster shot two other men that were with Wharton and killed one of them. They must have been trash or they would not have been in the company of the "thug," but they were not wanted by the law at that time and Rooster was criticized. He had many enemies. Pressure was brought and Rooster made to surrender his Federal badge. We knew nothing of it until it was over and Rooster gone.

He took his cat General Price and the widow Potter and her six children and went to San Antonio, Texas, where he found work as a range detective for a stockmen's association. He did not marry the woman in Fort Smith and I supposed they waited until they reached "the Alamo City."

From time to time I got bits of news about him from Chen Lee, who did not hear directly but only by rumor. Twice I wrote the stockmen's association in San Antonio. The letters were not returned but neither were they answered. When next I heard, Rooster had gone into the cattle business himself in a small way. Then in the early 1890s I learned he had abandoned the Potter woman and her brood and had gone north to Wyoming with a reckless character named Tom Smith where they were hired by stock owners to terrorize thieves and people called nesters and grangers. It was a sorry business, I am told, and I fear Rooster did himself no credit there in what they called the "Johnson County War."

In late May of 1903 Little Frank sent me a cutting from *The Commercial Appeal* in Memphis. It was an advertisement for the Cole Younger and Frank James "Wild West" show that was coming to play in the Memphis Chicks' baseball park. Down in the smaller type at the bottom of the notice Little Frank had circled the following:

HE RODE WITH QUANTRILL!
HE RODE FOR PARKER!

Scourge of Territorial outlaws and Texas cattle thieves for 25 years!
"Rooster" Cogburn will amaze you with his skill and dash with the six-shooter and repeating rifle! Don't leave the ladies and little ones behind! Spectators can watch this unique exhibition in perfect safety!

So he was coming to Memphis. Little Frank had teased me and chaffed me over the years about Rooster, making out that he was my secret "sweetheart." By sending this notice he was having sport with me, as he thought. He had penciled a note on the cutting that said, "Skill and dash! It's not too late, Mattie!" Little Frank loves fun at the other fellow's expense and the more he thinks it tells on you the better he loves it. We have always liked jokes in our family and I think they are all right in their place. Victoria likes a good joke herself, so far as she can understand one. I have never held it against either one of them for leaving me at home to look after Mama, and they know it, for I have told them.

I rode the train to Memphis by way of Little Rock and had no trouble getting the conductors to honor my Rock Island pass. It belonged to a freight agent and I was holding it against a small loan. I had thought to put up at a hotel instead of paying an immediate call on Little Frank as I did not wish to hear his chaff before I had seen Rooster. I speculated on whether the marshal would recognize me. My thought was: *A quarter of a century is a long time!*

As things turned out, I did not go to a hotel. When my train reached "the Bluff City" I saw that the show train was on a siding there at the depot. I left my bag in the station and set off walking beside the circus coaches through crowds of horses and Indians and men dressed as cow-boys and soldiers.

I found Cole Younger and Frank James sitting in a Pullman car in their shirtsleeves. They were drinking Coca-Colas and fanning themselves. They were old men. I supposed Rooster must have aged a good deal too. These old-timers had all fought together in the border strife under Quantrill's black standard, and afterward led dangerous lives, and now this was all they were fit for, to show themselves to the public like strange wild beasts of the jungle.

They claim Younger carried fourteen bullets about in various portions of his flesh. He was a stout, florid man with a pleasant manner and he rose to greet me. The waxy James remained in his seat and did not speak or remove his hat. Younger told me that Rooster had passed away a few days before while the show was at Jonesboro, Arkansas. He had been in failing health for some months, suffering from a disorder he called "night hoss," and the heat of the early summer had been too much for him. Younger reckoned his age at sixty-eight years. There was no one to claim him and they had buried him in the Confederate cemetery in Memphis, though his home was out of Osceola, Missouri.

Younger spoke fondly of him. "We had some lively times," was one thing he said. I thanked the courteous old outlaw for his help and said to

James, "Keep your seat, trash!" and took my leave. They think now it was Frank James who shot the bank officer in Northfield. As far as I know that scoundrel never spent a night in jail, and there was Cole Younger locked away twenty-five years in the Minnesota pen.

I did not stay for the show as I guessed it would be dusty and silly like all circuses. People grumbled about it when it was over, saying James did nothing more than wave his hat to the crowd, and that Younger did even less, it being a condition of his parole that he not exhibit himself. Little Frank took his two boys to see it and they enjoyed the horses.

I had Rooster's body removed to Dardanelle on the train. The railroads do not like to carry disinterred bodies in the summertime but I got around paying the premium rate by having my correspondent bank in Memphis work the deed from that end through a grocery wholesaler that did a volume freight business. He was reburied in our family plot. Rooster had a little C.S.A. headstone coming to him but it was so small that I put up another one beside it, a sixty-five-dollar slab of Batesville marble inscribed

REUBEN COGBURN
1835–1903
A RESOLUTE OFFICER
OF PARKER'S COURT

People here in Dardanelle and Russellville said, well, she hardly knew the man but it is just like a cranky old maid to do a "stunt" like that. I know what they said even if they would not say it to my face. People love to talk. They love to slander you if you have any substance. They say I love nothing but money and the Presbyterian Church and that is why I never married. They think everybody is dying to get married. It is true that I love my church and my bank. What is wrong with that? I will tell you a secret. Those same people talk mighty nice when they come in to get a crop loan or beg a mortgage extension! I never had the time to get married but it is nobody's business if I am married or not married. I care nothing for what they say. I would marry an ugly baboon if I wanted to and make him cashier. I never had the time to fool with it. A woman with brains and a frank tongue and one sleeve pinned up and an invalid mother to care for is at some disadvantage, although I will say I could have had two or three old untidy men around here who had their eyes fastened on my bank. *No, thank you!* It might surprise you to know their names.

I heard nothing more of the Texas officer, LaBoeuf. If he is yet alive and should happen to read these pages, I will be pleased to hear from him. I judge he is in his seventies now, and nearer eighty than seventy. I expect some of the starch has gone out of that "cowlick." Time just gets away from us. This ends my true account of how I avenged Frank Ross's blood over in the Choctaw Nation when snow was on the ground.

Afterword

DONNA TARTT

It's commonplace to say that we "love" a book, but when we say it, we really mean all sorts of things. Sometimes we mean only that we have read a book once and enjoyed it; sometimes we mean that a book was important to us in our youth, though we haven't picked it up in years; sometimes what we "love" is an impressionistic idea glimpsed from afar (Combray . . . madeleines . . . Tante Leonie . . .) as opposed to the experience of wallowing and plowing through an actual text, and all too often people claim to love books they haven't read at all. Then there are the books we love so much that we read them every year or two, and know passages of them by heart; that cheer us when we are sick or sad and never fail to amuse us when we take them up at random; that we press on all our friends and acquaintances; and to which we return again and again with undimmed enthusiasm over the course of a lifetime. I think it goes without saying that most books that engage readers on this very high level are masterpieces; and this is why I believe that *True Grit* by Charles Portis is a masterpiece.

Not only have I loved *True Grit* since I was a child; it is a book loved passionately by my entire family. I cannot think of another novel—any novel—which is so delightful to so many disparate age groups and literary tastes. Four generations of us fell for it in a swift *coup de foudre*—starting with my mother's grandmother, then in her early eighties, who borrowed it from the library and adored it and passed it along to my mother. My mother—her eldest granddaughter—was suspicious. There wasn't much overlap in their reading matter: my gentle great-grandmother—born in 1890—was the product of an extremely sheltered life, and a more innocent creature in many respects than are most six-year-olds today; whereas my mother (in her twenties then) kept books like *The Boston Strangler* on her bedside table. Purely from a sense of duty, she gave *True Grit* a try—and was so crazy about it that when she finished it, she turned back to the first page and read it all over again. My own middle-aged grandmother (whose reading habits were rather severe, running to politics and science and history) was smitten by *True Grit*, too, which was even more remarkable since—apart from the classics of her childhood, and what she called "the great books"—she didn't even care all that much for fiction. I think she might have been the person who suggested that it be given to me to read. And I was only about ten, but I loved it too, and I've loved it ever since.

The plot of *True Grit* is uncomplicated, and as pure in its way as one of the *Canterbury Tales*. The opening paragraph sets up the premise of the novel elegantly and economically:

> People do not give it credence that a fourteen-year-old girl could leave home and go off in the wintertime to avenge her father's blood but it did not seem so strange then, although I will say it did not happen every day. I was just fourteen years of age when a coward going by the name of Tom Chaney shot my father down in Fort Smith, Arkansas, and robbed him of his life and his horse and one hundred and fifty dollars in cash money plus two California gold pieces that he carried in his trouser band.

The speaker is Mattie Ross, from Yell County near Dardanelle, Arkansas, and the time is the 1870s, shortly after the Civil War. Mattie leaves her grief-stricken mother at home with her younger siblings and sets out after Tom Chaney, the hired man who has killed her father. ("Chaney said he was from Louisiana. He was a short man with cruel features. I will tell more about his face later.") But Chaney has joined up with a band of outlaws—the Lucky Ned Pepper gang—and ridden out into the Indian Territory, which is under the jurisdiction of U.S. Marshals. Mattie wants someone to go after him; and she wants someone who will shoot first and ask questions later. So she asks the sheriff in Fort Smith for the name of the best marshal he knows:

The sheriff thought on it a minute. He said: "I would have to weigh that proposition. There is near about two hundred of them. I reckon William Waters is the best tracker. He is a half-breed Comanche and it is something to see, watching him cut for sign. The meanest one is Rooster Cogburn. He is a pitiless man, double-tough, and fear don't enter into his thinking. He loves to pull a cork. Now L. T. Quinn, he brings his prisoners in alive. He may let one get by now and then but he believes even the worst of men is entitled to a fair shake. Also the court does not pay any fees for dead men. Quinn is a good peace officer and a lay preacher to boot. He will not plant evidence or abuse a prisoner. He is straight as a string. Yes, I will say that Quinn is about the best they have."

I said, "Where can I find this Rooster?"

Movie fans will call to mind the aging John Wayne, who famously portrayed Rooster Cogburn on the screen, but the Rooster of the novel is somewhat younger, in his late forties: a fat, one-eyed character with walrus mustaches, unwashed, malarial, drunk much of the time. He is a veteran of the Confederate Army; and, more particularly, of William Clarke Quantrill's bloody border gang, notorious in American history for the massacre at Lawrence, Kansas, and also for launching the careers of the teenaged Frank and Jessie James. Mattie runs Rooster to ground in his squalid rented room at the back of a Chinese grocery store. "Men will live like billy goats if they are let alone," she remarks, disapprovingly and he's happy enough to take Mattie's money to ride out after her father's killer—but not to let Mattie come along.

> He sat up in the bed. "Wait," he said. "Hold up. You are not going."
> "That is part of it," said I.
> "It cannot be done."
> "And why not? You have misjudged me if you think I am silly enough to give you a hundred dollars and watch you ride away. No, I will see the thing done myself."

Mattie is not the only party after Tom Chaney; so is a vain, good-looking Texas Ranger named LaBoeuf who has already tracked Chaney over several states. LaBoeuf (whose name is pronounced "La Beef," and who is somewhat overly proud of his membership in the Rangers) wants to team up with Rooster to bring Chaney back alive and collect the bounty. But the dandy LaBoeuf, clanking along in his "great brutal spurs" and "Texas trappings," is no more interested than

Rooster in allowing a fourteen-year-old girl to tag along on a manhunt; moreover, LaBoeuf's intent is to bring Chaney back to Texas to hang for shooting a Texas state senator in a dispute over a bird dog, a claim which Mattie hotly disputes:

"Haw, haw," said LaBoeuf. "It is not important where he hangs, is it?"

"It is to me. Is it to you?"

"It means a good deal of money to me. Would not a hanging in Texas serve as well as a hanging in Arkansas?"

"No. You said yourself they might turn him loose down there. This judge will do his duty."

"If they don't hang him we will shoot him. I can give you my word as a Ranger on that."

"I want Chaney to pay for killing my father and not some Texas bird dog."

"It will not be for the dog, it will be for the senator, and your father too. He will be just as dead that way, you see, and pay for all his crimes at once."

"No, I do not see. That is not the way I look at it."

Not surprisingly, Rooster and LaBoeuf contrive to slip away from Fort Smith without Mattie. But she strikes out after them; and as hard as they ride, they cannot lose her. ("What a foolish plan, pitting horses so heavily loaded with men and hardware against a pony so lightly burdened as Blackie!") Finally, when they cannot get Mattie to turn back, they accept her: first, in anger, as a worrisome tagalong; then, grudgingly, as a mascot and equal of sorts; and at last—as she stands among them and proves herself—a relentless force in her own right.

Like *Huckleberry Finn* (or *The Catcher in the Rye*, or even the Bertie and Jeeves stories for that matter) *True Grit* is a monologue, and the great, abiding pleasure of it that compels the reader to return to it again and again is Mattie's voice. No living Southern writer captures the spoken idioms of the South as artfully as Portis does; but though in all his novels (including those set in the current day) Portis shows his deep understanding of place, *True Grit* also masters the more complicated subtleties of time. Mattie, having survived her youthful adventure, is recounting her story as an old woman, and Portis is such a genius of a literary mimic that the book reads less like a novel than a first-hand account: the Wild West of the 1870s, as recollected in a spinster's memory and filtered through the sedate sepia tones of the early 1900s. Mattie's narrative tone is naïve, didactic, hardheaded, and completely lacking in self-consciousness—and, at times, unintentionally hilarious, rather in the manner of Daisy Ashford's *The Young Visiters*. And like *The Young Visiters* (which is largely delightful because it views the most absurd Victorian crotchets as obvious common sense), a great part of *True Grit*'s charm is in Mattie's blasé view of frontier America. Shootings, stabbings, and public hangings are recounted frankly and flatly, and often with rather less warmth than the political and personal opinions upon which Mattie digresses. She quotes scripture; she explains and gives advice to the reader; her observations are often overlaid with a decorative glaze of Sunday School piety. And her own very distinctive voice (blunt, unsentimental, yet salted with parlor platitudes) echoes throughout the reported speech of all the other characters—lawmen and outlaws alike— to richly comic effect, as when Rooster remarks austerely of a young prisoner he has brought back alive to stand trial: "I should have put a ball in that boy's head instead of his collarbone. I was thinking about my fee. You will sometimes let money interfere with your notion of what is right."

Mattie is often compared to her literary ancestor, Huckleberry Finn; but though the two of them share some obvious similarities, in most respects Mattie is a much harder customer than careless, sweet-tempered Huck. Where Huck is barefoot and "uncivilized," living happily in his hogshead barrel, Mattie is a pure product of civilization as a Sunday school teacher in nineteenth-century Arkansas might define it; she is a straitlaced Presbyterian, prim as a poker. "I would not put a thief in my mouth to steal my brains," she says coolly to the drunken Rooster; tidy, industrious, frugal, with a head for figures and a shrewd business sense. Her deadpan manner is reminiscent of Buster Keaton: Mattie, too, is a Great Stone Face; she never cracks a smile when recounting the undignified and ridiculous situations in which she finds herself; and even predicaments of great danger fail to draw violent emotion from her. But this deadpan flatness serves a double purpose in the novel, for if Mattie is humorless, she is also completely lacking in qualities like pity and self-doubt, and her implacable stoniness—while very, very funny—is formidable, too, in a manner reminiscent of old tintypes and *cartes des visites* of Confederate soldier boys: dead-eye killers with rumpled hair and serious angel faces. One cannot picture Huckleberry Finn in the same light; for while Huck is an adventuresome spirit, duty and discipline are wholly foreign to him; conscripted by any army, any cause, he would desert in short order, slipping away the first chance he got to his easy riverbank life. Mattie on the other hand is the perfect soldier, despite her sex. She is as tireless as a gun dog; and while we laugh at her single-mindedness, we also stand in awe of it. In her Old Testament morality, in her legalistic and exacting turn of mind, in the thunderous blackness of her wrath—"What a waste! . . . I would not rest easy until that Louisiana cur was roasting and screaming in hell!"—she is less Huck Finn's little sister than Captain Ahab's.

True Grit is an adventure story, and though the two books in most respects could not be more different, Mattie's quest in some ways reflects Dorothy Gale's in *The Wizard of Oz*. Practical Dorothy, throughout all her trials, is really only working her way back home to Kansas; while practical Mattie, with her own mission and her own brace of unlikely travelling companions, is riding in the historical shadow of a very different Kansas: the mythical outlaw territory of Quantrill and his Confederate raiders. While Quantrill—a brilliant tactician—was romanticized in some quarters as an outlaw chieftain a la Alexandre Dumas, the massacre he led at the abolitionist town of Lawrence, Kansas, is considered the worst atrocity of the American Civil War, and history has tended to view Quantrill as a cold-blooded killer. (One man—shot five times when he tried to surrender—was left for dead by his assailant with the parting advice: "Tell old God that the last man you saw on earth was Quantrill." Rooster, presumably, has come by some of his famous meanness under Quantrill's tutelage; the incident with Odus Wharton and the bodies in the fire does seem to have some parallels with unpleasant incidents in historical accounts of raids at Lawrence and Centralia; and certainly he has picked up Quantrill's reputed habit of riding against his enemy with the reins of his horse between his teeth and a revolver in each hand. And yet it is scoundrelly old Rooster who—like Huck Finn, revolting instinctively against the accepted brutality of his day—rises unexpectedly to *True Grit*'s moments of justice and nobility. He does this in a number of minor comical respects (as in his satisfying encounter with the two "wicked boys" who are tormenting the mule on the riverbank) not to mention the novel's extraordinary climax. But perhaps the most gratifying moment in the entire book is when Rooster is jolted from his ambivalence about Mattie by the sight of LaBoeuf falling upon her with a switch:

I began to cry, I could not help it, but more from anger and embarrassment than pain. I said to Rooster, "Are you going to let him do this?"

He dropped his cigarette to the ground and said, "No, I don't believe I will. Put your switch away, LaBoeuf. She has got the best of us."

"She has not got the best of me," replied the Ranger.

Rooster said, "That will do, I said."

LaBoeuf paid him no heed.

Rooster raised his voice and said, "Put that switch down, LaBoeuf! Do you hear me talking to you?"

LaBoeuf stopped and looked at him. Then he said, "I am going ahead with what I started."

Rooster pulled his cedar-handled revolver and cocked it with his thumb and threw down on LaBoeuf. He said, "It will be the biggest mistake you ever made, you Texas brush-popper."

True Grit, in short, begins where chivalry meets the frontier—where the old Confederacy starts to merge and shade away into the Wild West. And without giving anything away, I can say that the book ends at a travelling Wild West show in Memphis in the early 1900s: which is to say, at once in the twentieth century and firmly enshrined in myth and legend.

True Grit was first published in 1968. When it came out, Roald Dahl wrote that it was the best novel to come his way in a long time. "I was going to say it was the best novel to come my way since . . . Then I stopped. Since what? What book has given me greater pleasure in the last five years? Or in the last twenty?" Certainly when I was growing up in the 1970s, *True Grit* was widely thought to be a classic; when I was about fourteen years old, it was read along with Walt Whitman and Nathaniel Hawthorne and Edgar Allen Poe in the Honors English classes at my school. Yet (because, I believe, of the John Wayne film, which is good enough but which doesn't do the book justice),

True Grit vanished from the public eye, and my mother and I, along with many other Portis fans, were reduced to scouring used bookstores and buying up whatever stock we could find because the copies we lent out so evangelically were never returned. (In one particularly dark moment, when my mother's last copy had disappeared and a new one was nowhere to be had, she borrowed the library's copy and then pretended that she had lost it). Now—thankfully—the book is back in print, and I am delighted to have the honor of introducing Mattie Ross and Rooster Cogburn to a new generation of readers.

Center Point Publishing
600 Brooks Road • PO Box 1
Thorndike ME 04986-0001 USA

(207) 568-3717

**US & Canada:
1 800 929-9108**
www.centerpointlargeprint.com